*He grabbed her by the elbow
and pulled her close.*

Then give me my payment now. Kiss me,
and that will prove to you how much you
love me."

She yanked away. "No! I will pay you anything else,
but you can't make me feel what I do not feel! What
else shall I pay you to make things square between
us? Name your price, but it will not be me!"

He laughed bitterly, scornfully. "I don't know.
Why don't I take your firstborn child?"

"Ha!" she cried. "Don't be ridiculous!"

"What price would *you* have me name?"

"Fine, then! My firstborn child it is. And when I
have money, I will mail it to you and we will be clear
of each other, all debts paid, over and done with."

Bertie suddenly felt that she had to get away from
him. It was urgent that she not listen to another word
he had to say. Overcome with emotion, she ran up
the stairs into the alley.

ONCE UPON A TIME

The Crimson Thread

SUZANNE WEYN

SIMON PULSE
New York   London   Toronto   Sydney

SIMON PULSE

An imprint of Simon & Schuster Children's Publishing Division

1230 Avenue of the Americas, New York, NY 10020

Copyright © 2008 by Suzanne Weyn

All rights reserved, including the right of reproduction in whole or in part in any form.

SIMON PULSE and colophon are registered trademarks of Simon & Schuster, Inc.

For information about special discounts for bulk purchases, please contact Simon & Schuster Special Sales at 1-866-506-1949 or business@simonandschuster.com.

The Simon & Schuster Speakers Bureau can bring authors to your live event. For more information or to book an event contact the Simon & Schuster Speakers Bureau at 1-866-248-3049 or visit our website at www.simonspeakers.com.

The text of this book was set in Adobe Jenson.

Manufactured in the United States of America

6 8 10 9 7

Library of Congress Control Number 2008922278

ISBN 978-1-4169-5943-4

For my parents, Theodore Weyn and Jacqueline Weyn, with thanks for raising me on stories of immigrant grandparents and great-grandparents as well as longtime New Yorkers. These stories, some heartrending, others hilarious, (some having both qualities at the same time) were so vividly told that they have found their way into every line of this novel.

PROLOGUE

Once upon a time, I believe it was 1880 or there-abouts, a young princess set sail from Ireland for a faraway land. Bridget O'Malley never knew she was of royal lineage, due to the reduced circumstances into which she was born.

Foreign conquest had brought endless brutal war to the land, and the devastation of this strife, coupled with the dire poverty it left in its wake, had long ago vanquished the line of magical druidic priestesses and high kings from which Bridget was descended. Though she did not appear the part in her rags and cloddish, peat-covered boots, Bridget O'Malley was, indeed, a princess, and, on her mother's side, a distant but direct descendent of the high king Cormac mac Airt of legend.

For anyone with eyes to see, her lineage should have been clear enough. She carried the brilliant, orange-red crown of vibrant, unruly curls that marked all the royal women of her line. She had the unmistakable crystal blue eyes and the spray of freckles across her high cheek-bones.

As Queen Avriel of the Faerie Folk of Eire, I have watched these disowned royals, these noble spirits without crowns, for centuries too numerous to count. A descent in fortune may obscure royal lineage in the eyes of mankind, but not so in the realm of Faerie. Here we know that true royalty remains in the blood regardless of fortune's deviations. And so I watch and record the royal ones, despite the fluctuating cycles of rise and fall that they may experience.

Bridget and Eileen O'Malley were my special concern. After their mother died, Bridget and her wee sister were the last princesses of their line. In my ancient *Book of Faerie* their histories were recorded with no less attention than when their kinswomen of times past wore the Celtic crowns on their heads.

Bridget and little Eileen's lives were hard from the start, and then the Great Hunger struck. When the potato crop failed, the already-dire starvation, poverty, and crushing serfdom spun wildly out of control. The famine left mothers to die in their thatched cottages, their frozen babes blue in their arms. Between 1846 and 1850 droves of starving, desperate families set sail for distant shores. They went to lands known as Canada, Australia, Great Britain, and a place called America. Hundreds of them left, their meager belongings in tow, not knowing what lay ahead, but praying it would be better than the crushing life they'd had.

When Bridget's mother died, her father, Paddy O'Malley, decided that the time had come to do as so many of his neighbors and kin had already done. He would take his children to America.

And so—invisible to all—I went too, in my role as faerie historian. A strange fate awaited Princess Bridget. I never would have predicted the turns of events that she encountered, being unfamiliar with the magic of foreign lands as I was at the time. For the mix and tumble of exotic magic she experienced was like nothing I could have imagined; nor could have Bridget.

And thus begins this faerie's tale.

CHAPTER ONE
A Brave New World

As she made her way down the steamer's gangplank, Bridget O'Malley cradled three-year-old Eileen, her younger sister, in the crook of her bent arm. Eileen snored lightly, her head nestled on Bridget's shoulder, her blond curls like a cloud around her peaceful, round face.

With her other hand, Bridget gripped a battered suitcase. It contained everything she had managed to acquire during her seventeen years in the world: two skirts, one of them patched and short, coming just above the ankle, the other, longer one with two rows of ruffles on the bottom, each row added as she grew; a worn-soft plaid flannel nightgown; a few sets of bloomers and undershirts; two faded blouses; a horsehair brush; a blue satin ribbon; a chipped hand mirror; a green and tan blanket of homespun Irish wool crocheted by her mother shortly before her death a year earlier; and two somewhat dull sewing needles.

Bridget squinted against the fierce sunlight. The strong ocean breezes pried strands of curls loose from her upswept hairdo and flung them into her eyes. Setting down the suitcase, she brushed the corkscrews of hair aside.

"Best not let that case stray from your hands, my girl," her father, Paddy O'Malley, advised brusquely in his thick Irish brogue as he stomped down the ramp, flanked by his three sons, nineteen-year-old Finn, thirteen-year-old Seamus, and eleven-year-old Liam. "We've come to the land of thieves and pickpockets."

"Ha!" Bridget let out an ironic laugh. "And here I was thinking this was the land of *opportunity*. I believe it was you, your very self, who told me so, was it not? Let me think . . . how many times have I heard it?"

"Only a hundred," Finn put in, a smile in his green eyes as he set down one end of the steamer trunk containing all their household belongings and Seamus put down the other. Heeding his father's warning, Finn kept one worn boot propped on top of the trunk.

"No, surely it was two hundred, at least." Seamus continued the joke. He removed his wire-rimmed glasses and gave them a quick wipe on his shirt.

"A thousand times!" Liam piped up. He had the same red curls as Bridget, but his eyes were a vivid green and they sparkled with mischief now, lit gleefully with the fun of teasing their father. "I'm sure he's said it exactly one thousand times."

"Yes, I believe you're right, Liam," agreed Bridget

with a grin. "'*Land of opportunity*'—I believe I *have* heard that phrase *exactly* a thousand times."

"And so it is!" Paddy O'Malley insisted, taking his children's teasing in stride. He gazed around at the other passengers who streamed from the ship. They were disheveled and exhausted from the long, cramped trip, dragging trunks and baskets containing all their earthly belongings. Paddy looked on them with benevolent pride, despite their tattered appearance. In his eyes they were kindred spirits, bold seekers of a better life who were now teetering on the brink of incipient riches.

"It is a great land, indeed, and we will find our fortunes here," he said confidently. "But in the meantime, be wary. Keep your wits about you at all times."

Bridget smiled at him as the six of them moved forward with the crowd entering the building. This was a strange new world, and they'd have to learn its ways as fast as possible.

But what could be more auspicious than to arrive at the very entrance of a castle? The Castle Garden immigrant processing center was, indeed, very like a castle. In fact, it had been a fort against the British back during the American War of 1812. It stood at the southern tip of New York City, with two grand rivers on both sides and the very ocean at its door. The glistening building dazzled Bridget with its expansive entryway, elaborate scrollwork, and surrounding wall. Beside the doorway, an American flag flapped in the wind.

They joined the crowd of people moving inside to the great, round center room with its high domed ceiling. "Saints be praised," Bridget muttered under her breath, awed at the sight of the massive room. Even the village church back in Ballinrobe had nothing as grand as this ceiling supported by impossibly thin columns.

They got on one of the many lines and crept forward until they finally reached a desk where a uniformed official sat at a desk with a big ledger on it. Along with her father and brothers, Bridget signed her name in the book, relieved that they didn't ask her to write anything else. Her name was all she knew how to write.

Crumpling his tweed cap nervously in his large, rough hands, Paddy produced a letter from the traveling country doctor attesting that the family was free of disease. He'd made sure to acquire this letter, having heard far too many stories of others who'd endured the grueling sea passage only to be turned back or, at the very least, stuck in quarantine because their health was suspect.

"Address?" barked the official behind the desk, a scowling, thin-lipped man, without looking up from the papers he was filling out.

Paddy O'Malley took a slip from his jacket pocket and showed the official the address written on it: 106 Baxter Street. His best friend from home, Mike O'Fallon, had been kind enough to rent an apartment for them using money Paddy had sent him. "Mike O'Fallon assures me that it's a fine place," Paddy told the official, "the best he could get for the dollars I sent him."

"The Five Points, eh?" the man said with a grunt as he glanced up for the first time. "Why am I not surprised?"

"Pardon? The what?" Paddy O'Malley asked.

"The intersection of three blocks creates five corners, so they call the area the Five Points. It's the part of downtown you people all seem to head for," he stated with a derisive nod at the others on line. "You can walk there from here; I guess that's why you all go there."

"Are there many others from Ireland there, then?" Paddy inquired hopefully.

"Years ago you people controlled the whole rat-infested slum," said the man, returning to his paperwork. "There was nobody there but a ton of Irish along with a few Black Africans. But now they're pouring in from Italy, Germany, and all parts of East Europe. You've even got Chinese and Jewish down there nowadays. But don't fret. You'll still find boat-loads of Irish there."

Paddy nodded, though a look of worry crossed his face. Bridget understood it. Italians! Germans! Africans! Jewish! Chinese! She didn't even know what an Eastern European was! None of the O'Malleys had ever seen a person who wasn't Irish, let alone someone all the way from China.

The official glanced up for a second time as he

handed Paddy a cardboard billfold of entry papers. "You and your boys might find work at the Paper Box Factory at Mission Place," he advised. "And your girl here should check with the House of Industry on Worth Street. They can direct her to the uptown families looking for servants."

"She'll not be a servant," Paddy disagreed confidently, "not one as skillful as she is with a needle."

"Suit yourself," said the official. "Many women go into the needle trades, but she'll have to post a one-dollar deposit with any employer she wants to work for."

"One dollar!" Bridget gasped. Where would that come from? She wasn't even sure how much money it was, but it sounded like a lot.

"That's how it's done. It's why girls hire out as servants," the man said gruffly.

With a nod, Paddy motioned his family to move away from the desk with him. They followed him a few paces until he stopped and faced them. His ruddy face erupted into a brilliant smile. "We did it! We're in!" he exulted.

"Where to now, Da?" Seamus asked.

"On to 106 Baxter Street," he told them excitedly, his face beaming. "The kind gentleman there says it's but a hop, skip, and jump from here. Let us be off. Our fortunes await us!"

CHAPTER TWO
The Crimson Thread

Eileen had awakened during the walk to Baxter Street and now stared around, wide-eyed, as the family trudged up the five flights of narrow tenement stairs. Bridget held tight to her small hand as they struggled up the dimly lit stairway.

Some apartment doors were open, and inside they could see dim, dreary spaces. Dirty, half-naked children overflowed from some of the open doors, and the hallway exploded with the sounds of life being lived at top volume, sometimes in languages they could not understand.

"Gaa, what is that stink?" asked Seamus, his face twisted in disgust.

"I think it's cabbage cooking," Finn suggested.

Bridget sniffed the stale air. She recognized the cabbage, but there were other food smells that were completely unfamiliar. And there were odors intermingled that she didn't think were food at all.

"Are you sure it's cabbage?" Seamus questioned. "It smells like dead bodies to me."

"When did you ever smell dead bodies?" Finn challenged with a snort of dark laughter.

"I helped Alice Feeney turn her granddad over, and he had been dead in the sheep pen nearly two days when we found him," insisted Seamus with grim pride. "Ew, he was foul."

"Seamus would do *anything* for Alice Feeney," Liam taunted.

A faraway wistfulness leaped into Seamus's eyes. "It's true, I would have, but I guess I'll never get the chance now."

"Don't despair, my lad," Paddy encouraged his son as he stopped in front of a closed door and checked the number on the keys the landlady had given him. "You will return to Ballinrobe as a rich man someday, and you'll whisk lovely Alice away in your fine carriage."

Bridget shook her head in amusement. Her da was a dreamer, to be sure, and his big ideas weren't always realistic ones. But his exciting imaginings had given them all something to hold on to, so she was glad he was the way he was.

Paddy turned the key and opened the door. "Home, sweet . . ." His voice trailed off into stunned silence as the O'Malley clan took in the awful sight of their new home.

The apartment was a one-room rectangle, filled with strewn garbage and abandoned belongings from the previous tenant. The faded beige walls were chipped, with large holes in some spots. The wood-planked floor was broken clear through in places.

The kitchen was in the main room. Several of its cabinet doors hung from their hinges. In a corner was a two-burner gas stove, but no sink; nor was there a bathroom. "I suppose we share the utilities," Paddy ventured gamely. "I saw a sink in the hall. We passed it just now."

Those things didn't bother Bridget. At home they'd had to go outside to pump water and use the outhouse behind the cottage, even on the coldest days, so in a way, this indoor plumbing amounted to an improvement on that situation. What did bother her were the squalid filth of the place and the stench of the garbage from the other apartments.

A rush of claustrophobia mixed with panic threatened to overwhelm her. How could she live with this unremitting ruckus and stench? Desperately needing air, she threw her weight into the sash of the only small window in the place, trying to lift it. "Help me, Finn," she demanded when it wouldn't budge.

Finn put his shoulder into it but quickly discerned the cause of its refusal to move. "It's painted shut," he announced.

The room suddenly felt unbearably airless and foul. It swirled in front of her eyes, and she could feel the blood draining from her face.

Water! She needed water. And air!

Rushing from the room, she ran down the hall, searching for the sink Da had referred to. It was deep and chipped but a welcome sight. She braced herself against it and began to pump. Instead of the sparkling well water she was used to, rusted liquid trickled down. It was disgusting, and she couldn't stand to drink it.

The faint feeling threatened to overtake her, so she sat on the floor to avoid falling and injuring herself, letting her head hang between her knees. Maybe she was simply tired from the many days at sea. But this was not what she had expected, not at all.

"So you like New York City. I can tell," said a thickly accented male voice in a mocking tone dripping with irony.

Lifting her head, she took in the slim man leaning against the wall across from her. He wore baggy trousers belted at the waist with a worn leather strap and an equally baggy white shirt with the long sleeves rolled to the elbows. His forehead was wide under wild, thick dark hair. She wondered if his flat, crooked nose had ever been broken. She decided it must have been, for she'd seen broken noses before.

Bridget estimated that he might be twenty, maybe a little younger. The world-weary hardness in his dark eyes struck her as inconsistent with the high-strung energy evident in his leanly muscular frame.

The hallway had gone oddly quiet, as if, having cooked and eaten their meals, everyone had retired early for the evening, even though the late summer sun still filtered through the grimy hall windows. The apartments that moments ago had teemed with life were now closed and erupted in only occasional bursts of loud conversation.

The young man stepped forward so that he was in front of the filtered sun shining in from a small hallway window. It haloed his form, making him seem surrounded by an unearthly haze and throwing his face into shadow. It also now required her to squint against the light when she looked up at him.

He tossed her something small, and, reflexively, she raised her hand to snatch it out of the air. It was a red and white mint wrapped in wax paper. "Sometimes a little sugar is all you need," he said. "Don't you think so, princess?"

She stared at him sharply. Why had he called her *princess*? How could he know that it was her secret fantasy—that she was somehow royal despite all the evidence to the contrary?

He couldn't. She was being ridiculous; it must be her overactive imagination again.

"Is something wrong?" he asked.

His accent was so thick. Where was he from? She had never known anyone who spoke like this.

"No, nothing. I'm sorry; it's nothing." Looking down, she undid the mint's wrapper but hesitated before popping it into her mouth. Hadn't Da warned them to be wary? Who knew what was in this mint?

Bridget wrapped the mint up again with the

intention of returning it. Despite the kindness of the gesture, the fellow unnerved her.

When she raised her head to speak to him, he was gone.

In the morning they unbundled the last of their supply of cheese and bread and had it for breakfast. Then, using the tools Paddy had brought with him, they began work on the tenement apartment, scraping the walls, fixing the cabinets, and repairing the planks in the floor.

While Da and the older boys worked, Bridget and Liam hauled in buckets of water and did their best to scrub everything down. "Don't be playing in that," she had to scold Eileen again and again, as the little girl insisted on splashing in the rusty water.

Finn chiseled into the paint sticking the window shut. Once it was opened, the sounds of the street below poured into the place.

Unlike the quiet countryside that they'd come from, the clatter of horses' hooves on the cobblestone streets, the squeak and grind of wagon wheels, the call of the pushcart peddlers selling their wares, and the din of chattering people were relentless. "See?" said Paddy brightly. "Mike O'Fallon wouldn't let us down. He found us the finest place in all the Five Points."

Bridget, Seamus, Finn, and Liam exchanged dubious glances. "*This* is the finest place they've got?" Seamus asked, and then he burst into laughter at the sheer absurdity of the idea. His hilarity proved contagious, and soon they were all convulsed in peals of laughter, even Paddy. Eileen, not getting the joke, clapped her small hands and laughed along with the rest. She finished off by splashing exuberantly in the wash bucket, drenching herself and causing even more laughter.

By midday they were famished. It suddenly struck them that there was no goat to milk or hen's nest to raid for eggs. Paddy took out his small leather pouch of coins. "Go down to the street and see what you can get for this," he instructed Bridget, placing a twopence in her palm.

"Won't I need American money?" she questioned.

He shrugged. "Try to find a peddler from the old country. He might want to be sending it home to his family."

Bridget climbed down the five flights of stairs and went again into the busy street. It was mobbed with people who seemed to think nothing of bumping into her and pushing her aside in their hurry.

Peddlers called out, advertising their wares. The variety of things they had for sale was impressive: fiddle strings, suspenders, pocketbooks, used clothing, even rags. They had items for sale that she couldn't even name because she had never seen them before.

The food-selling carts were farther down the block. Before she reached them, she lingered a moment over several carts selling sewing needles, buttons, and thread. The variety of texture and color in the threads was astounding. One spool stood out from the rest, almost throbbing with vivid energy. The silken thread was a vibrant crimson red.

"How much for that thread?" she impulsively asked the peddler. Surely she couldn't buy it, but she asked nonetheless, not sure why she had spoken.

The man had been counting out some bills and looked up at her, slightly startled. "What's that, Bridget?"

She gasped. "How did you know my name?"

The peddler laughed, not unkindly. "I could tell from your Irish voice, your brogue. That's what we call all you Irish girls—Bridgets. What can I do for you, Bridget?"

She pointed at the thread. "How much?"

"A dollar a yard. It's from China and worth every penny." He looked her over, assessing her ability to pay his price. "It's more than I'm guessing you have."

An American dollar waved in front of her eyes. "Give her a yard of the crimson thread."

Bridget whipped around to see the same strange young man from the day before. "No, no, please," she declined. "I couldn't take it. I have no need for—"

Too late.

The thread was measured, snipped, and wrapped around a wooden spool.

The peddler handed it to the young man, who then pressed the spool of thread into Bridget's hands. "Crimson red is a royal color. It suits you," he said.

He looked into her eyes, and she felt he was seeing every secret thought, every doubt, every hidden longing she had ever harbored. She felt shaken to her core.

"I cannot accept this," she said softly.

He didn't take his eyes from hers as he replied, "Someday you will pay me back." With that, he turned away from her and disappeared into the crowd.

CHAPTER THREE
The Fighting O'Malleys

Work at the Paper Box Factory kept the family from starving that first week, but Paddy and the boys loathed it. Paddy, Finn, and Seamus were used to working the fields, but as backbreaking as that work was, they discovered that they preferred it to the airless, hot, cramped factory where they were constantly harassed and upbraided by a foreman to work faster.

"The most miserable landlord back home never spoke to me the way that foreman does. I don't know who he thinks he is," Paddy complained almost daily.

"The guy on the loading dock keeps calling me Mickey," reported Finn angrily. "He calls anyone who is Irish, Mickey. I'd like to punch him."

Seamus, whose job was to fold and stack boxes from the moment he arrived until he left in the evening, never had much to say. He usually fell asleep almost immediately, sometimes curled on the floor, still in his boots.

"Poor thing," Bridget remarked to Finn one evening when she watched Seamus snoring on the floor. A boy of only thirteen shouldn't be working so hard."

"It won't kill him," Finn said as sat on his mattress, sewing a button back on his shirt. "I was working the farm with Da at thirteen."

Bridget sighed uncertainly. "Somehow it's not the same."

"Can I work when I'm thirteen?" asked Liam eagerly from a corner of the apartment, where he and Eileen had been watching a spider crawl across the floor.

"Pipe down and don't be rushing it," Finn chided him mildly. "Working is no great joy, not the kind of work we're doing."

"Maybe when you're thirteen we can have you in school," Bridget added hopefully.

After two weeks of unsuccessful searching, Bridget found work as a seamstress in a private shop run on the top floor of a tenement down the street. Finn had found the notice advertising for seamstresses in the local paper and directed her to it.

She hated having to leave Liam home in charge of Eileen. He was so young to be stuck with babysitting duty all day. But what other choice did she have? "Now you have a job—taking care of Eileen," she said as she went out the door for her first day at work.

He waved away her remark dismissively. "This isn't a job."

"Well, it's a big help, anyway," she insisted, giving both Eileen and Liam a kiss.

"Bridgey, don't go!" pleaded Eileen, wrapping her arms around Bridget's neck.

"I have to," she said, slipping from the frowning child's grasp. "You be a good girl for Liam, and I'll be home at suppertime." She hurried down the stairs, worried and unhappy to be leaving an eleven-year-old boy in charge of three-year-old. It wasn't fair to either of them.

She found the address and showed the owner, Mrs. Howard, her worn sewing needles and told her honestly that she had learned to sew from her mother and that she sewed all her family's clothing.

"You'll be doing handwork, so I won't need a deposit against breakage of one of my sewing machines," said Mrs. Howard, a stern-faced woman. "I'll expect you to use your own needles."

"Thank you so much, ma'am," Bridget said, feeling incredibly lucky. "When should I start?"

"Right now," Mrs. Howard said, gesturing toward a narrow flight of stairs leading to the top floor.

Bridget's new job was to sew men's vests in a windowless room with about twenty other women. There were only five sewing machines, which the older, more experienced women used to sew men's caps and shirts. Everyone else was relegated to doing handwork. Bridget was eager to learn the machine and hoped she could get a chance someday.

They were paid by the item, so it was in their best interest to put their heads down and work hard. This, combined with the claustrophobic atmosphere and the heat of the crowded space, kept conversation to a minimum. There were occasional eruptions of gossip and other talk, however.

A slightly plump, darkly pretty girl named Maria, with big brown eyes and curly, nearly black hair, just a few years older than Bridget, sat beside her. "I saw you in the street once before, you know. I remember your hair. *Bellissima!* You are so lucky. Some Italians have red hair too. They're mostly from the north, though. My family is from the south, so I have this dark hair, same as everyone else."

"Red hair is not so uncommon in Ireland," Bridget told her without looking up from her sewing.

"I know that. I've seen other Irish redheads," Maria replied. "Their hair isn't as beautiful as yours."

"You're very kind. Thank you," said Bridget, blushing just a little from the praise.

"I saw you talking to that Ray Stalls," Maria continued.

"Who?"

"By the sewing supply cart. You were talking to him."

"His name is Ray Stalls?" Bridget asked, trying not to sound too interested.

"That's what he calls himself," said Maria, "but that can't possibly be his name, can it?"

"Why not?" Bridget inquired. Why should Maria think it wasn't his real name?

"You've heard him talk!" Maria said. "No one who talks with such a thick accent is named Ray Stalls. He's made that name up to be more American."

Bridget's lips parted in surprise. "Can you do that?"

Maria threw her head back and laughed. The disturbance made the other women look their way. Some scowled at them, others smiled.

"Of course you can change your name, silly," Maria said, whispering this time to draw less attention. "People do it all the time here in America. Sometimes the officials do it for you."

"What do you mean?" Bridget asked. "Someone changes your name?"

"It happens all the time," Maria confirmed. "My name is Maria Papa. That's the right name, because the official at Castle Garden wrote it correctly on my papers. But I have cousins in this country named Pope, and Popa, and Papal. The officials made a mistake on their papers, so now they have new names."

"That's terrible."

Maria shrugged her shoulders resignedly. "It's not so bad. New country, new name. But a name like Ray Stalls—he made that up. He just wants to make people believe he's a real American. Or maybe . . ." She scooted her chair closer and dropped the volume of her voice conspiratorially. "Maybe he's hiding from someone."

Bridget replied in an equally hushed tone. "Who would he be hiding from, do you think?"

"Use your imagination," Maria urged. "He could be escaping a wife or even the law; maybe he's a fugitive from the government of his country, a political exile."

"What country would that be?" Bridget wanted to know. In the last three days she'd realized how incredibly naive and uninformed she was regarding the other peoples of the world. It made her feel very young and stupid; such feelings were new and unwelcome sensations to her.

"I don't know," admitted Maria.

"He's German," an older woman with snowy white hair in a bun informed them sharply, glancing up for a second from her machine. Her name was Hilda, and her accent was the same as the one Ray Stalls had.

"What's his real name?" Maria asked boldly.

"I don't know. Nobody knows," the woman replied. "Sometimes he lives in the basement of my building along with the other men who pay two cents a night for a spot to sleep. They're like animals, packed in so tight."

"But I met him in *my* building," said Bridget.

"Ach!" the woman grunted gutturally with an irritated wave of her thick hand. "Who knows where he goes or what he is up to? He seems to be

Suzanne Weyn

everywhere. You girls stay away from him. He is trouble."

Bridget sat forward in her chair, interested. "Why do you say that? What kind of trouble?"

"He disappears for days on end, and then suddenly he is back," the woman told them. "He reads books, dangerous books full of wild ideas. I hear that he shoots off his big mouth in the saloons. Someday he'll go too far and they will ship him out of here. It is called deportation. In this country if you are an immigrant and you make the government mad . . ." She smacked her hands together briskly. "Poof! You are gone." She jerked her thumb over her shoulder. "They ship you out."

By the end of her first day, Bridget was weary to the bone. Her shoulders ached from hunching over her sewing, and there was numbness in her legs from sitting for so long. She had completed only two vests in eight hours. But at twenty-five cents a vest, she felt rich with a fifty-cent piece in her pocket.

On the way home, she stopped at a vegetable cart for five potatoes and then entered a butcher shop to get a beef bone for soup. When she'd made her purchases, she had twenty cents left. Stopping for a small glass bottle of milk for Eileen brought it down to fifteen cents.

Still, having money in her pocket and a bag of food to show for her day's work made Bridget forget about her aches. Her footsteps felt light as she hurried up the five flights to her apartment.

22

She arrived to find Liam on all fours, barking and pretending to be a dog chasing Eileen. The little girl ran in circles, shrieking with laughter, shouting, "Doggie! Doggie!"

Bridget put down her bag of groceries and scooped Eileen up in her arms. "Is the mad dog chasing you?" she asked playfully.

"Doggie!" cried Eileen, pointing at Liam, who barked in response. "Liam is funny!"

Bridget circled around the nearly empty apartment, not eager to sit again so soon after her day in a chair. "How did it go today?" she asked Liam.

He lay spread-eagled on the wooden floor. "All right, I suppose, but it's tiring taking care of a baby."

"I not baby!" the girl objected. "I this many," she added, holding up three fingers.

Bridget rubbed the back of her hand tenderly along Eileen's cheek and glanced at Liam sympathetically. "I suppose you really should be in school, shouldn't you? It's bad enough that Seamus is shut up in that box factory all day."

"I wouldn't mind school. I want to read, like Finn. But who would take care of her if I went to school?" he replied, lifting his chin toward Eileen.

"That's the problem," she admitted. "I'll go down to the mission soon as I can to find out if there's anything to be done about it. Maybe there's someone who cares for little children around here, and as soon as I earn some money we can hire her. That would let you go to school. They have free schools here, you know."

Setting Eileen on the floor, she crossed to the stove and lit it. A few pieces of sooty coal had been left from the previous tenant, and they had piled the broken floorboards inside to supplement it. "You know, I hear that a lot of tenement apartments don't even have a stove," she told Liam. "And some still have outdoor toilets that everyone in the building must share and only one sink on the ground floor. Mike O'Fallon really did find us a good place."

She knew she was stretching the truth. This tiny, dilapidated apartment wouldn't be any sane person's idea of good, and she completely understood the skeptical glance that Liam was now directing her way; nonetheless, she felt good and thought it was important to spread her optimism. What good would it do them to cave in to despair?

"What are you cooking?" Liam asked.

"As soon as these burners get hot, I'll make a soup from potatoes and a beef bone." She was pulling a patched tin pot from the cupboard when Paddy, Finn, and Seamus burst in the front door. Underneath Paddy's right eye was a spreading purple welt. Finn's collar was torn, and his lip was swollen and caked with blood. Seamus's cheek had been scraped, and the right lens of his glasses had a crack in it. "What happened?" she cried when she saw the condition they were in.

"I knew one day that foreman would push me too far," Paddy growled.

"You've been there less than a week," she reminded him.

"Yes, well, it's been too long," he grumbled. "Him calling us Mickey this and Mickey that. I could take it, but when he started picking on Seamus, and him but a boy—well, I just snapped."

"And you snapped too?" she asked Finn, taking in his disheveled appearance.

"I had to back Da up, didn't I?"

"I suppose," she agreed.

"It was great!" Seamus put in enthusiastically. "Da laid the guy out. Everyone was laughing at him. He had it coming, and they were glad to see him go down."

"You were lucky you didn't get arrested," she said as the reality of what they were telling her settled in. She remembered Hilda telling them how immigrant troublemakers were sent home . . . "deported" was the word she had used.

Her father and brothers glanced at one another sheepishly. "We ducked out the back door as the coppers were coming in the front," Finn told her. "We don't think they know where we live."

"But they know your names," she pointed out.

"Well, yeah," Finn admitted.

"Don't worry your head, my girl," said Paddy, sitting and mopping his grimy brow with a piece of torn cloth from his pocket. "We were fighting with right on our side."

She was of two minds as she stood there. Part of

her wanted to scold such rash behavior. There was clearly no going back to the place. They were paid at the end of the week, so there would be no pay coming this week for the work they had already done. Her pay alone couldn't carry them.

But another part of her felt too proud of them to scold. They were defending Seamus, so it was the right thing to do. They'd stood up for him and for their self-respect.

"Tomorrow I'll go out and find a new job, a better job," Paddy assured them.

"It might be good if we traveled out of this neighborhood to look," Finn suggested, "just in case the coppers are looking for us. It wouldn't hurt to stay out of sight."

"We're wanted men," said Seamus with a grin that showed that his front tooth had been chipped in the scuffle.

"Ah, Seamus, your glasses are broken, as is your beautiful smile," Bridget lamented.

"I don't mind. I can still see out of my glasses, and my smile was too perfect. Now I look like a real man," he replied.

"You *are* a real man," Paddy praised Seamus, at the same time ruffling his hair as he would do to a young boy. "You did the O'Malley name proud today. But you're right, Finn, tomorrow we'll venture uptown in our pursuit of new employment." He turned to Bridget. "And if anyone asks you if you know Paddy, Finn, or Seamus O'Malley, you never heard of us."

"You disreputable lads are total strangers to me,"

she agreed with a wicked chuckle. But she rubbed the back of her neck as she laughed, a habit she had picked up from her mother. The two of them always did it when something was troubling them and they hadn't yet found the words to articulate their dismay.

CHAPTER FOUR
Rick Miller from Wales

That night Bridget lay on the straw mattress in her corner of the apartment with her eyes wide open, too worried to sleep. The lumpy bed was on the floor and was covered with the crocheted blanket her mother had made. They had ripped one seam of her shorter, patched skirt and used it to make a sort of curtain around her bed to give her some privacy.

She shared the bed with Eileen, who now lay asleep but was tossing fitfully. Bridget worried that the little girl hadn't eaten enough. The soup had not been as filling as she'd hoped, and Eileen had spilled half the precious bottle of milk before it was finished. Her small, round belly rumbled as though a wild creature were hidden inside.

Moonlight shone in from the one window, streaming above the curtain and illuminating the place where she lay. Her mind raced with plans. What would happen if her father and brothers did not find work? What if they were arrested? She didn't even have enough money to bail them out of jail or pay any fines. Da had long ago spent any money he'd brought on food and repairing the apartment. And whatever else happened, they could not allow themselves to be deported. Having sold nearly all they had in order to get to America, they would be in worse shape than before if they were forced to return to Ireland.

Maybe she could get Mrs. Howard to allow her to bring materials home. That way she could sew more vests at night and bring up her pay. It still wouldn't be enough, though.

For the first time since arriving, she wished they'd never left Ireland. She longed to be home in her bed with her window up, listening to the night wind rustling the bushes.

It didn't seem to matter anymore that they'd been poor and had often gone to bed empty-bellied. Now, in memory, the plain, thatched cottage became an airy, sunlit kingdom resplendent with shining, smiling faces—a palace of warm familiarity. It had been home, *her* home, and now it seemed like a priceless world, forever lost to her.

Exciting and new though it was, this place was *not* her home. It was strange, with brutal foremen, sweating women laboring in an airless attic, and an unsettling, mysterious young man who apparently read "dangerous books" and who seemed able to peer into her very heart.

There in the dark, stuffy room, the illumination from the moon shifted slightly, falling onto the top of her battered suitcase, which she was using as a makeshift night table. She had piled her few things on top of it. In the silver gleam, the spool of crimson thread seemed to pulse with its intense color, almost as if the moon had converted it into a living thing.

Bridget sat up with her back against the wall and picked up the spool of silken thread, shifting it from hand to hand, recalling how she'd acquired this small treasure. She looked at the vendor's stamp on the top of the spool that gave his name. "It comes from China," he had said. *Such a long way to travel*, she reflected, wondering if one of the Chinese people that she noticed on the streets had brought it.

Why had the thread caught her attention that day, almost as though it had called to her? It was beautiful, there was no doubt of that, and like many young women, she liked beautiful things. But there was something more to it that she could not quite figure out. Her unexplainable attraction to the thread had felt almost supernatural, like a prophecy waiting to be fulfilled.

Nonsense, she thought, putting the spool back on the suitcase.

She was only making up stories again with her wild imagination. Da always warned her against letting her fancies get the better of her.

As a child she'd often been sure that she had seen faeries and the little people darting among the trees.

Her mother had told her it was a sign of royal blood, this ability to see the faerie folk. But Da had quickly squelched that notion, advising against filling Bridget's head with ideas of royal blood and other nonsense.

His warning had come too late, though.

Her head had already locked onto the belief that she had a secret identity that no one else could see. She felt it deep inside with a confidence born of certainty. If she had ever voiced this idea, others would not only have mocked her but seen it as a sign of the most ridiculous arrogance, if not total lunacy; so she kept her secret unspoken.

Bridget was jolted from these ruminations when Eileen's eyes suddenly opened wide. For a brief moment the child appeared startled to be awake, and then her face crumpled into a mask of unhappiness. She began to whimper pathetically, pointing to her mouth, which she sometimes did when she was hungry.

It broke Bridget's heart to see her so hungry and to have no food for her. "I'm sorry, sweetie pie, I have nothing . . ." She suddenly remembered the mint that Ray Stalls had given her on the first day they'd arrived. She'd emptied it from her pocket when they had decided to use her skirt for a curtain.

Finding the candy, still wrapped, on top of her suitcase end table, she licked the sugary morsel cautiously. It tasted sweet, not like poison. Still . . . maybe it was too risky to give to the child.

Eileen continued to whimper pitifully until Bridget couldn't stand it anymore. The mint was probably fine. Her crazy imagination was simply spinning wild tales for her again. Why deprive the child?

"Here, baby, suck on this candy," she said. "Come to me, sit on my lap. I'll rock you back to sleep."

Eileen rolled over and crawled up onto Bridget's lap. Laying her head of soft curls on Bridget's chest, she held the striped candy to her mouth and seemed soothed.

Bridget began humming strains of a lullaby her mother had sung to her as a little girl. The homesickness it brought her was almost too much to bear, but it calmed Eileen to sleep.

As Bridget's eyes also drifted shut, she took the last of the mint from Eileen's sticky hands, fearing she might choke on it in her sleep. She slipped the sticky shard of leftover candy between her lips just moments before a dreamless slumber claimed her.

"Our fortune is at hand!" Paddy announced joyfully the next evening as he burst into the apartment.

"What happened? Why are you so late?" Bridget asked. She stood by the black stove with Eileen at her side. Finn, Seamus, and Liam lounged around a milk crate set up as a card table, fanned cards in hand.

"You are looking at J. P. Wellington's new carriage driver and stable manager!" Paddy's smile spread from ear to ear. "Meet Rick Miller!"

"Wha?" asked Seamus, looking up from his cards.

"Attend to me now, children," Paddy demanded as Eileen came to his side and he lightly tickled her belly. "This is a great and glorious day!"

"You're as puffed as a rooster," Bridget remarked with a touch of irritation. She'd passed another long, hard day in Mrs. Howard's steaming attic. The woman had found fault with the second vest she'd produced and ripped out the seams, paying her only a quarter for one vest. It had been barely enough for potatoes and another small bottle of milk. Bridget was exhausted and in no mood for guessing games or riddles. "Who is what's-his-name Wellington and this Miller?"

"I am Rick Miller," Paddy announced, beaming.

His children shot concerned, darting glances at one another in complete bewilderment. What was he talking about?

"He's gone delusional," Seamus suggested flatly.

"Have you been drinking, Da?" asked Finn, scowling with concern.

"How can you ask me that, I who have pledged to my parents, your grandparents, to stay ever sober? No I have *not* been drinking."

"Then it's as I said, he's lost his mind," Seamus insisted.

The look of wounded offense on Paddy's face remained there for only the briefest moment before erupting again into an irrepressible grin of satisfaction. "You children think you're so smart, but here's the long and short of it." He settled himself into their one chair and tugged at his trousers as he always did when preparing to tell a lengthy tale.

The boys put down their cards and regarded their father attentively. Bridget scooped up Eileen, balancing her on her right hip while leaning against the stove.

"Finn and I took ourselves uptown early this morning, as you well know," Paddy began. "We parted ways somewhere around Twenty-third Street. I continued on another ten blocks or so to a wide avenue know as Park Avenue, where I discovered an amazing world of houses, each one a small palace unto itself. And there I saw a sign reading 'Stableman wanted.' I carried myself in and applied for the job."

"What do you know about being a stableman?" Finn asked skeptically. "Nothing, I would venture to guess."

"You don't know everything about me, my boy," Paddy replied. "As a young man, before any of you were born, I spent time down Connemara way, a place renowned for its excellent ponies and fast horses. There I ran a stable for a Lord Pennyfather. During my job interview with J. P. Wellington's man, I recalled enough about horses from those days to convince the man that I knew my way around a stable. As a result, I am now the stableman and driver for J. P. Wellington."

"Is he a real rich guy? Did you meet him?" Liam asked eagerly.

"He is indeed a respected and wealthy captain of industry in the American style. I did not meet him, as he is, at present, touring his textile factories in the distant south of this sprawling country."

Though Paddy had not seen the inside of the elegant home, he had been dazzled by the carriage house with three fine horses and a splendid carriage. A separate small but refined room in the carriage house was for the stableman. It was now to be Paddy's room.

"How does this Rick Miller figure into your tale?" Bridget questioned.

"In a most American way," he replied, with a seasoned storyteller's air of relishing a delicious mystery about to be revealed. "During the course of his several letters to me, Mike O'Fallon warned that Americans exhibited a certain resistance to employing the Irish; as if the hardship and poverty we have endured has somehow rendered us disreputable."

"So *that's* why everyone kept turning me away today," Finn realized bitterly. "They all seemed interested in taking me on until the moment I opened my mouth."

"No doubt," Paddy agreed. "So, knowing this, I called myself Rick, which is the same as the end of my name, Patrick; and Miller, being near to the name O'Malley in sound. Rick Miller—it's close enough to my real name that at least I'll remember to answer to it."

"How did you explain the way you talk?" Bridget asked.

"I said I was a Welshman," he revealed with a self-satisfied shrug. "I don't think Wellington's man ever met a Welshman, so he had no idea what one might sound like. I told him Wales was a part of Great Britain, and that was good enough for him."

Paddy slapped his hands together robustly, a sign that his tale had ended. "What's to eat?"

"We saved you half a boiled potato and a glass of milk," Bridget told him. "It was the best I could do. Mrs. Howard wouldn't pay me for one of my vests. She said the seams were shoddy, but I think she was just letting me know that she's the boss and can do as she pleases."

"Have no care about it," Paddy assured her. He pulled a slim stack of American bills from his pocket. "It is the habit of J. P. Wellington to advance his workers the first two days' pay to see them through until the end of the week—the sure sign of a great and beneficent employer. Tonight we eat at Sullivan's Tavern. We'll dine in the rear quarters, so Bridget and Eileen can join us."

"Why can't I be in the front of the place?" Bridget asked indignantly.

"The front of a saloon is no place for a proper young woman or a child," Paddy stated firmly. "It's fit only for the rough talk and hard-drinking ways of men."

"Is it wise for us to go out in public," Finn questioned, "after what happened yesterday?"

"Another compelling reason to dine in the rear," Paddy slyly agreed.

CHAPTER FIVE
The Police Close In

The plate of short ribs, mashed potatoes, and carrots that Bridget ate at Sullivan's Tavern that night nearly brought tears of happiness to her eyes. She had been half-hungry for so long that she had forgotten what it was like to feel full. "I've never tasted anything so wonderful," she said, mumbling with her mouth full.

The tavern's back room, though plain with wooden tables, white unadorned walls, and a rough-hewn, wide-plank floor, seemed the height of luxury after so much deprivation. Every table was filled with people involved in animated conversation as they enthusiastically devoured their meals. Here and there, clusters of men and women stood talking, mugs in hand, periodically erupting in laughter. The atmosphere was raucous but reminded Bridget of a great wedding party she'd once attended as a little girl.

She grinned at Eileen, who sat in front of her

stew with her blue eyes beaming happily. There would be no growling, hungry beast in her small tummy tonight.

"So, shall we be calling ourselves the Miller family from now on?" Seamus inquired, his glasses steamed by the mist rising from his beef hash.

"Perhaps we should," said Paddy thoughtfully.

"I'll not be known by some foolish, made-up American name," Finn objected. "O'Malley is our family name going back for generations in County Cork. If we renounce it, we cut all lines with our past."

"It might help you get a job," Liam pointed out. "You could say you're a Walsh, though I'm still unclear as to why they would like a Walsh better than an O'Malley. I had a friend named Thomas Walsh, and he was no smarter than me."

"Welsh," Bridget explained, suppressing a laugh. "Da claimed he was from Wales, where the people are called Welsh."

"Oh," Liam said, nodding. "Finn, tell them that you're a Welsh."

"I'll never," Finn insisted firmly. "I'm Irish and proud of what I am."

"As am I," agreed Paddy, "but this is a new world and modern times; it requires a fresh attitude. We are beginning a new clan lineage. We are still who we are, but now we are the Irish-American branch of the clan."

Finn waved off his father's words with a dismissive swipe of his hand. "You don't believe that."

"I do!" Paddy insisted.

"You said you were Welsh!" Finn exploded indignantly. "You claimed your name was Miller. That's not even a Welsh name! It's American!"

Paddy pounded the table irately, rattling the glassware, his patience finally exhausted. "Those are trivial details, Finn! False pride will get you nowhere, boy! This new day requires a resourceful nature. Behold this abundance in front of you. This is what comes of ingenuity and quick thinking."

Bridget watched them intently. Finn and her father were so different. She wondered if the bit of schooling Finn had received had made the difference, or if they simply had differing natures. But maybe not so different, she considered. They were both proud, softhearted, and stubborn, and both had big dreams, just *different* dreams. Da wanted to be an American and make a new life, while Finn clung to his roots. She wondered if this was something they would ever be able to resolve.

Where did she stand on the matter? She wasn't sure. It seemed to her that there might be a way for a person to do both things at the same time—become this new thing, an American, while not denying your past. Maybe she was a dreamer too, to think she could have it both ways.

"My name means William," Liam said thoughtfully. "I could be William Miller, Willie Miller." He grinned, appearing fond of the idea.

"You could be Billy Miller," Seamus suggested.

"Billy Miller," echoed Liam, snapping his suspender straps with jaunty exuberance. "I like it."

"Don't be giving him ideas," Finn scolded Seamus.

"Why not? A kid told me that my name means James," Seamus replied unflinchingly. "Jim! Jimmy Miller! I've been thinking on it, and to me it sounds good. I don't think that foreman would have been so quick to whack someone named Jimmy Miller across the face."

Bridget could see both points of view. Since Finn was the oldest, she'd always followed his lead, but she didn't know if he was right about this. If taking on American names and ways helped them to eat regularly . . . it didn't seem so terrible.

A shot of animal awareness jolted her from these concerns. With darting eyes, she surveyed the crowded, noisy room of people eating at their tables, suddenly sensing that someone was staring at her. In a moment she found the source of her uneasy feeling.

Ray Stalls stood by the door, talking with five other rough-looking men. They were conversing boisterously and he was nodding, but his eyes were locked on her.

For an electric moment, they connected.

Then, ruffled by the audacious boldness of his brazen stare, she averted her gaze from his and looked down at her meal. She reviewed the sight of him in her mind's eye. In the company of the other burly men, he seemed slight and dark, his course curls tumbling into his fierce eyes; and yet there was something rough and attractively masculine about him, despite the fact that he was not much taller than she.

As she stared at her food, she became aware that the din of the place had quieted to a more subdued tone. Glancing up, she saw that her father and brothers were slumped in their seats. Da wore the desperate expression of a trapped fox. A purple vein above Finn's eyebrow throbbed with anxiety.

Two uniformed police officers had entered the tavern and now walked attentively among the tables, surveying each customer, clearly searching for someone, their intimidating billy clubs intentionally conspicuous under their arms.

They were searching for Da and the boys, she was sure. Her heartbeat quickened, the only part of her body not paralyzed with fear.

Sensing the air of deep unease in the room, Eileen's small brow furrowed into a scowl. She began to whimper, drawing everyone's attention, including that of the steely-eyed, suspicious officers. "There, there, sweetheart," Bridget soothed in a whisper, rubbing the girl's pudgy, stew-smeared hands. "Everything is fine. No need to cry."

For a brief moment, the officers studied the table where the O'Malley family sat, then exchanged knowing glances and approached.

Bridget's stomach clenched.

This was it.

Under the table, she grabbed Liam's quivering

hand. She could feel Seamus's knee trembling nervously, rocking the leg of the table. Would they take him in too? Really, he was only thirteen, just a boy.

Ray Stalls suddenly broke from his crowd of companions and lurched toward the officers.

Was he drunk?

It seemed so, the way he staggered so brazenly toward them. He stumbled and clutched the nearest officer in an effort to stay upright.

Still holding the officer's arm, he went down, spilling a pocketful of bills onto the floor as he went.

A gasp spread through the room at the sight of so much money.

"Pardon me," Ray Stalls said with a distinctly drunken slur, blurring even further the words so heavily accented with German. "Ssso sorry."

"Where did the likes of you come upon all this cash?" demanded the officer upon whose arm Ray Stalls had fallen.

Ray grinned foolishly at him. "An in-in-heritance, I assure you." He pulled himself unsteadily to his feet. "I am sssoo glad you men are here. Would you be kind enough to esh-esh-escort me to my home?" He threw his arm on the officer's shoulder, leaning heavily against him while he gazed around furtively with the expression of a man driven mad by paranoia. "The shtreets are f-f-full o' thieves, you know. I would be honored t' pay handsomely f'r your protec . . . shun."

Greed lit the faces of both officers.

"Gather your money, then," the second officer told him. "And wait here a moment."

He approached the O'Malley table. "Are you Patrick, Finn, and Seamus O'Malley?" he asked harshly.

Bridget could barely hear his words through the pounding of her heartbeat. She lifted Eileen from her chair and rocked her, ostensibly to soothe the child but just as much to settle her own nerves.

"No, officer, we are the Miller family, newly arrived from Wales," replied Paddy.

"Sure you are," the officer scoffed. "And I'm Sherlock Holmes."

"Pleased to meet you, Mr. Holmes," Paddy said, not catching the sarcasm in the officer's voice.

"Thomas, he's leaving," the first officer alerted the one at their table.

Ray Stalls was staggering to the front door, drunkenly clutching his cache of bills to his chest. The other customers looked on avariciously, not daring to move, as single bills fluttered, unnoticed by him, onto the floor.

The officer named Thomas looked torn between making his arrest of the brawling O'Malleys and attaining his portion of the cash they would surely get from the wealthy drunken fool hovering at the door. "Don't any of you leave until we return," he commanded the O'Malleys. "And be assured, we *will* be right back."

Ray Stalls banged the door open and staggered out into the night. The two officers jogged after him.

Paddy was instantly on his feet, throwing down dollars to cover the cost of the meal.

"Come on! Come on!" he urged his children.

"Maybe we shouldn't go home," Finn suggested.

"Perhaps not," agreed Paddy.

"Where would we go?" Liam asked.

Paddy thought, shifting anxiously from foot to foot. "Bridget, you return home with Eileen and Liam," he instructed her in whispered, rapid-fire words. "If they come for us, say we've run off and abandoned you with the children. If you need us, we'll be hiding in the carriage house of J. P. Wellington at Park Avenue and Thirty-third Street. But for the time being, forget you know that. I'll find a way to be in touch."

"Hurry! Hurry!" she urged them, moving the stunned Seamus out of his chair. "We'll be fine. Hurry!" In the next minute, her father and brothers were fleeing out the door and into the dark alley.

CHAPTER SIX
Fired!

It didn't help matters that the next day was the hottest Bridget had ever experienced. Mrs. Howard's attic sewing factory was a steaming sweatbox. "I didn't know I was coming to the tropics," she complained to Maria in a whisper, only to be shushed by the other women. The heat was doing bad things to their boss's temper, and they didn't want to risk crossing her for fear that she would rip out their newly finished seams or find some other excuse to call their workmanship shoddy and not pay them.

When Mrs. Howard left the room, no doubt treating herself to an escape from the heat, Bridget arched her aching back, pushed her damp curls back on her forehead, and thought about Ray Stalls. She wouldn't have taken him for a drunkard; there was something too keenly alert in him for that. She recalled that Hilda had said he lived in her basement. Only the most destitute men slept there, yet he had claimed to have come into money. "Does Ray Stalls still live in your basement, Hilda?" she asked.

Hilda grunted, not looking up from her sewing machine. "I have no idea. Come to think of it, I have not seen him of late. Are you still daydreaming about that scoundrel?"

"I am not daydreaming about him," Bridget denied. "I was only wondering."

Mrs. Howard came through the door and locked Bridget in a steely glare. "Come with me, young woman," she instructed sternly. "Bring all your belongings, including your needles. You shall not be returning."

Bridget looked desperately to Maria. What was happening? "Are you firing her?" Maria demanded bravely.

"That is none of your concern," replied Mrs. Howard. "Come now, Miss O'Malley."

Bridget gathered her things and followed Mrs. Howard out. The woman dug into a change purse and handed her a dime. "This will pay you for the work you have done. Please leave now and do not bother to return tomorrow or any other day."

"But why?" Bridget demanded. "Was the vest I did yesterday so terrible? I promise you that today's work will be better." She did not want to lose this job. Despite this heat, from what she'd heard, it was better than any of the factories.

"It has nothing to do with your work. While I was just downstairs, a neighbor told me that the police were at your tenement asking about members of your family. As I understand it, they're wanted in relation to some sort of assault down at the box factory. I can't employ anyone who is in trouble with the law," she informed Bridget coldly.

"But I am not in any trouble," Bridget insisted. "It has all just been a misunderstanding."

Mrs. Howard let out a scornful and knowing chuckle. "I've heard that many times before. It's always a simple misunderstanding with you people. Please, go."

Bridget could see that there was no sense in pleading any further. The hard mask of finality on Mrs. Howard's face was impenetrable. Her cheeks burning with the unfairness of this humiliation, she descended the splintered stairs until she came out into the blinding sun of the bustling street.

She weaved through the crowd, once having to jump into the street as someone threw a bucket of gray wash water from a window above. When she returned to the sidewalk, she found that she'd stepped into a pile of horse dung. "Ah, saints take pity on me," she muttered angrily as she stopped on the corner to wipe the excrement from her boot. Could this day get any worse? She sincerely hoped not, although she knew it was entirely possible.

"Psst!"

The sound made her wheel around sharply to face the narrow alleyway from which the hiss had come. Seamus stood with his back pressed against the wooden building. With a quick check around, she darted into the alley. "What are you doing here?"

"I could say the same to you," he retorted. "Why aren't you at work? I didn't expect to see you so soon."

"I was fired," she told him. "Listen, you have to get out of here. The police are looking for you."

"Da sent me down to get you. There's a job for a girl who sews up at the grand house. You should see the place, Bridget! It's near to a palace."

"Let me go home and freshen up."

"No! He says you are to come right away. They've already interviewed a line of girls, but Da has told them that you are the finest seamstress in all of Wales."

"What did he tell them that for?" she cried.

"You know Da," was the only reply he needed to make. She certainly did! No doubt this was more of his so-called resourcefulness and quick thinking.

Together, Seamus and Bridget headed uptown. Along the way, he told her how Finn had run into a fellow Irishman he'd met at the box factory who had offered him work on a fire truck. "He didn't even have to pretend to be Welsh," he informed her enthusiastically. "The man said there's lots of Irish on the trucks these days. He said there were even beds where he could sleep and food at the firehouse. It's good Finn's going there, because you know Da and he have not been getting on since last night. Da says Finn's being a fool, and Finn says Da's not loyal to the old country."

Bridget shook her head regretfully. "They're both so stubborn. I'm sorry to see Finn go, but it sounds like a good opportunity."

"I'm about to have a good opportunity too," Seamus added eagerly. "Da is going to talk to them about taking me on as his assistant. I could learn to be a stableman and even a coachman eventually. There's decent money in that."

"Good for you," she praised him.

"I'd be living there with Da. Maybe you could live in the carriage house too. It smells of horses, but it's not a bad smell once you get used to it. All three of us could wind up living in the grand house. Da says they'd give you a room upstairs in the servants' quarters if you get the job. Think of that!"

"What about Liam and Eileen?"

"I don't know. Maybe we could bring them."

"Well, we'd have to. We can't just leave them behind now, can we? I wonder if they'd allow it." She breathed in a nervous, quavering breath. She certainly needed a job, but she was far from a fine seamstress.

Since arriving in America, she hadn't traveled out of the Five Points neighborhood. She'd thought the entire city looked the same, but as they continued uptown she became aware of how completely wrong she had been.

Well before they even reached Twenty-third Street, the streets became wider, which let in more sunlight. The people walking along were more orderly, staying to the clean, quiet sidewalks. The roads were paved with cobblestones rather than dirt, and they were not strewn with filth.

When they turned a corner, Bridget gasped and staggered back in surprise, clutching Seamus's thin shoulder. A giant copper hand, easily three stories or more high, jutted up above the trees in a park across the road, a gleaming copper torch clenched in its grip.

With her hand on her panting chest, Bridget laughed at her own frightened reaction. "Saints have pity, I didn't know what I was seeing at first," she said.

"It's part of a huge statue they will be building in the harbor," Seamus told her. "They have put the hand here just for the time being."

"It must be a colossal thing, this statue, to warrant a hand the size of that," she commented.

Seamus nodded as they hurried across the wide road toward it. Elegant men and women circled the impressive hand.

Bridget took in the attire of the fashionable uptown crowd. The women wore tall hats, somewhat similar to the ones worn by the men, but the female version of the hat came with ornate feathers, netting, bows, and veils festooned around them. The tailored bodices and slim skirts of their outfits created a narrow silhouette until they turned, revealing a bump under the frock that gave the impression that the wearer possessed an unnaturally large rear end.

They passed diagonally across the park and went a few more blocks until they came out onto Park

Avenue. "I don't know about this, Seamus," she said. "We don't belong in such a grand place."

There were no listing wooden tenement buildings here, no people lounging idly on stoops, no garbage overflowing from cans. Here the buildings were all made of glistening stone or brick. Uniformed doorman stood at attention atop each gated, high-stooped entryway. Potted plants and sculptures adorned the small but immaculately manicured front yards. Then they reached the home of J. P. Wellington.

"It's a palace," she murmured to Seamus as she stared up the steps, awestruck.

Bridget O'Malley had never in her seventeen years felt a stronger urge to run away.

CHAPTER SEVEN
Balancing Act

Paddy was waiting for her on the high, gated front steps of J. P. Wellington's luxurious Park Avenue townhouse, his expression eager. "This is good," he said. "I wasn't expecting to see you so soon, but I came out just now to check, just the same."

"She got fired," Seamus explained.

Bridget opened her mouth to tell him the story, but he cut her off. "It's fate," he said. "And it only proves that you were meant to get this position for which I have put you forward. Seamus, go water the horses for me. I am going inside to introduce Bridget to the head seamstress."

She began to climb the steps, but Paddy put his hand on her shoulder to stop her. "We go in the servants' entrance," he said, steering her down several steps to a plain doorway slightly below street level.

He whisked her through a kitchen bustling with

busy servants and up a narrow flight of stairs into the front hallway. He paused only long enough to whisk a piece of lace off an end table and draped it around her shoulders by way of improving her plain, sweat-stained blouse.

"Da, no!" she objected. "They'll recognize it."

"Nonsense! Do you think they know every piece of lace in this grand house?" he replied, adjusting the material evenly on her shoulders. "Button up your collar there."

He led her down the elegant hall with its sparkling crystal chandeliers overhead and thick, plush Asian rugs beneath until they came to a set of carved wooden doors whose brass handles had been polished to a rich gleam. Paddy banged on the door with his rough fist, and Bridget cringed a little. Surely this sort of thunderous noise was not fitting in such a fine and silent home.

"Enter," came a low-pitched voice.

The woman who sat behind the ornate desk in the study was possibly the thinnest woman she had ever seen who wasn't falling over faint from starvation. On the contrary, this woman seemed quite alert, with probing eyes below a wide forehead under a high nest of upswept gray hair.

"Allow me to introduce my daughter, the greatest seamstress New York will ever see, Bertie Miller!" Paddy announced in a booming voice as though she were the star attraction at some theatrical entertainment.

Bridget's head snapped around to stare at her father in surprise.

Bertie Miller?!

The greatest seamstress New York will ever see?!

"What sort of name is Bertie?" the woman asked, eyeing Bridget critically. "Is it . . . Welsh?"

"French by way of Wales," Paddy said. "It's short for Bertrille."

Amusement played in the woman's eyes. Unlike the man who had interviewed her father, Bridget had the distinct impression that this woman was not fooled for a moment. No doubt she knew an Irish brogue when she heard one. "Have you brought any samples of your work?" she asked.

"No," Bridget replied.

"All our things were lost at sea when the ship we were sailing was nearly shipwrecked in a storm," Paddy jumped in to explain.

Bridget couldn't believe she was hearing this latest fabrication, it was so wildly untrue. The entire trip had been days of dull, sometimes nauseating, rocking under a monotonously overcast sky without a drop of rain.

Paddy stepped forward, stretching out his arms proudly. "Fortunately, this very shirt I'm wearing survived the tempest. It was made by her hand."

Survived the tempest! Bridget tried not to let her face reveal her shock at this bold-faced lie. Her mother had made the shirt he wore! It was hard to accept that her father could be such an outrageous liar. But maybe that was too harsh. He was an avid storyteller, and all good tale tellers sometimes lost the line between truth and fiction. To him, anything might be true; it was only a matter of which version of the story he was telling. She almost had to laugh when she thought of how he objected to her flights of fancy, when she'd probably inherited her imaginative ways from him.

"Of course, she made this garment some years ago, when she was only a child," he went on. "But the workmanship has held up very well, weathered the storm beautifully. Come examine it for yourself."

The woman came out from behind the desk, revealing herself to be exceptionally tall. She examined Paddy's sleeves and collar. "It is indeed well done," she concluded.

"The girl is a wonder," Paddy went on. "Not only can she sew a perfect seam, but she can spin thread, tat lace, embroider, and weave. If you take her on, you will thank me for the rest of your days."

"Is that so?" the woman asked skeptically.

"Mark my words," Paddy assured her, deliberately missing the disbelief in her tone.

"I would work very hard and do whatever you want," said Bridget sincerely, hoping to bring some small sense of truth and reality into the proceedings.

"Have you any references?" the woman asked.

"We are newly arrived and this would be her first employment in America, and, as I mentioned, the many testimonies she brought from home were all lost at sea," Paddy said.

A tight, pinched smile formed on the woman's lined lips. "I see." She turned her attention to Bridget. "You will start as my assistant. I hope that is not too menial a position for one as gifted as yourself."

"No, ma'am, not at all," Bridget answered.

The woman nodded. "You may call me Margaret. I will call you Bertie. We will begin tomorrow morning at seven sharp and work until six in the evening. We will be making the clothing for Mr. Wellington's eldest son and his three daughters, who are fashionable young women."

"Yes, ma'am."

"Mr. Wellington's fortune has been made in the textile industry," Margaret continued. "Fabrics and clothing are of the utmost importance in this household. Your work must be beyond reproach. You are being taken on in a conditional capacity, subject to dismissal if your work does not meet my expectations. Is that clear?"

Bridget swallowed hard and immediately hoped the sharp-eyed Margaret hadn't noticed. She'd thought her clothes-making skills were sufficient until Mrs. Howard had ripped her vest apart. Now she was no longer as confident.

"Oh, you'll be more than happy with her work," Paddy interjected.

"I'm speaking with your daughter now, Mr. Miller," said Margaret. She returned her attention to Bridget. "Any number of girls have applied for this position. It is an excellent opportunity. You are being offered it based on your father's recommendation. Mr. Wellington believes in employing members of the same family. I suggest you do your utmost to make the most of this."

"Yes, ma'am."

"Will you be requiring a room?"

"Yes, she will!" Paddy answered for her.

"No, ma'am," Bridget disagreed. "We have little ones at home who require tending at night."

"Still, it would be good for her to have quarters in case she's ever required to stay late and work on important garments," Paddy insisted. "Work will always come first."

Margaret glanced uncertainly from father to daughter. "You may use the smallest maid's room on the top floor at the end of the hall. It will be cleared out for you by tomorrow, but you will be free to go home in the evening if you so choose, as long as you return promptly in the morning. I will tolerate no lateness."

"That's more than fair. Thank you," replied Bridget.

"And one more thing," Margaret added. "Please return that doily around your shoulders to the hall table before you leave."

Bridget flushed with mortification. Why did she let her father persuade her to do these things? "Yes, ma'am," she mumbled, not even able to meet Margaret's eyes.

"Very well, we will see you tomorrow," Margaret said, dismissing her.

Bridget turned and left through the tall wooden doors. When they were again in the hall, she exploded at her father in a furious whisper as she yanked the offending lace from her shoulders. "Why did you tell her I was an expert seamstress?"

He stepped back as though she'd struck him. "You should be all smiles and thanking me," he replied. "You got the job, didn't you?"

"And why did you tell her I needed a room? Have you forgotten about Eileen and Liam?"

"That room is important. You want to live here and become part of the household. Liam can go stay at the firehouse with Finn or board with me in my room in the carriage house. They won't even notice him."

"What about Eileen?"

A thoughtful, slightly guilty look passed across his face. "I saw Mike O'Fallon last night. He has a sister who lives upstate who might take her on for a bit."

"No!" Bridget objected forcefully. "Eileen stays with us. We're her family! I'll not have you fobbing her off on strangers. We wouldn't know how she was being treated. We might never get her back."

"That apartment costs money," Paddy reminded her. "I'm sure Mike's sister is a fine woman."

"Our apartment rent is paid to the end of the month, isn't it? So, we'll keep Liam and Eileen there until then, and I'll think of something in the meantime."

"All right," he agreed. "You three sleep there until the end of the month, and then we will discuss this again. At the moment, you might thank me for getting you this fine position."

"Thank you," she said as she put the piece of lace doily back onto the hallway table.

"How are you, my babe?" Bridget greeted Eileen as she came in the door almost an hour later. She scooped the girl into her arms.

Bridget saw that Eileen had been changed into a clean jumper. "You're doing a good job, Liam. Sorry you have to stay here all day. A boy of eleven should be in school. Go outside and play for a while. Da gave me a whole dollar for supper, so I bought a beef bone, vegetables, and milk for a proper supper, and there are three eggs for the morning, too."

"Thanks," said Liam, racing out the door.

She found the old food-stained jumper and, with Eileen toddling beside her, washed it in the hallway sink, wrung it, and headed back to the apartment. She set Eileen on their shared mattress with a rag doll she had fashioned for her. "You play here while I hang this on the fire escape to dry," she instructed her sister.

Shoving open the window, she climbed out onto the metal perch and hung the dripping cloth over the railing. The heat and clatter of the outside immediately assailed her. How different this world was from the one she had just left, and yet only blocks apart.

What would she wear to work tomorrow? What would the others in the household think of her in her shabby skirt and cloddish boots? She worried about the "fashionable" young daughters of J. P. Wellington. What would they be like?

"Are you lost in the American dream?"

"Huh! What?" she sputtered, startled from her thoughts.

Ray Stalls was slightly over her head and to her right, climbing down from the roof on the fire escape beside the one she was on.

"What are you doing out here?" she asked.

"I like to sit on the rooftops and read," he answered. "It's cooler up there. These fire escapes are new, you know. The government made the landlords put them in not more than ten years ago. Before that, when these wooden tenements started to blaze, you were trapped like a rat inside. The landlords don't care about the poor people who live in their buildings; they never would have put them in if they didn't have to. I find them convenient for getting around."

"What are you? Some kind of burglar?" she asked, thinking of the cash he'd produced the night before.

He chuckled scornfully. "If I were that, I would not be swinging around the monkey bars here in this neighborhood. What would I steal?"

She flushed slightly, admitting to herself that this was true. She felt foolish for not realizing it herself.

"Have you sobered up yet?" she asked.

He gazed at her with that steady, deep stare that so unnerved her. "Are you really that stupid?" he replied.

"I beg your pardon!" she exclaimed, scowling indignantly. "I'll not stand out here and be insulted by the likes of you, who go swinging around on a building in the early evening and who was seen staggering drunk the night before."

"I wasn't drunk, you silly girl," he stated, his mouth quirking up at the side in an ironic grin. "One of the men I was talking with told me that the cops were looking for your father and your brothers. You can thank me that the three of them are not rotting away over in the Tombs."

"The what?"

"Prison! At the very least they'd have sent them across the East River to Blackwell's Island to the workhouse for the drunk and disorderly. Who knows when they would have gotten back if they'd been sent there?"

"Why should I thank you for that?"

"Why do you think?" he countered cannily.

In truth, the reality of what had happened was dawning on her. He'd thrown himself on the police and enticed them with the sight of so much cash. Maybe he had even bribed them. "I see," she admitted. "Did it cost you much?"

He crowed with laughter. "Once I led them far enough away, I took off running." He swung around the rail of his fire escape and leaped lightly onto hers.

He stood there, balancing effortlessly on the railing.

The precariousness of his position left her speechless. "Do come down," she implored, "before you fall."

He dropped down easily in front of her. "I left them in the dust and kept my money," he boasted.

"And you risked all that for my father and brothers?" she questioned.

"No. I did it for you."

"Why?" she asked.

"Why do you think?"

Before she could say anything more, he once again flipped over the railing and scrambled away with an acrobat's ease.

CHAPTER EIGHT
In the Grand House

On her first day at J. P. Wellington's, Margaret showed Bridget to the room that would now be hers, on the top floor where the servants lived. It was large enough for just a narrow cot and a small dresser. The only view visible from its high, narrow window was that of blue sky. Still, it was immaculately clean and even smelled of lavender. "There on the bed is your dress and smock. I have visually estimated your size, a skill you will learn," Margaret told her. "Put it on and report to the sewing room on the floor below."

The outfit was a plain blue cotton dress with a loose-fitting, darker blue cotton smock over it. Simple as it was, it felt luxurious to her because it was clean and new.

The sewing room couldn't have been more different from Mrs. Howard's sweatshop. Sunlight streamed in through many opened windows. Wide tables were strewn with the most gorgeous fabrics she had ever seen. Four headless dressmaker's dummies were positioned throughout the rooms; three were female forms and one was a male of good height with broad shoulders. "Is this for Mr. Wellington's suits?" she asked Margaret.

"Mr. Wellington Junior," Margaret clarified as she seated herself behind a shiny black sewing machine with the name SINGER printed in cursive lettering on its side. "Mr. Wellington Senior has his suits made for him exclusively in London."

"How old is Mr. Wellington Junior?"

"He is eighteen," Margaret answered. "Now, enough chatter. This morning I am making a gown for Miss Elizabeth, and you will assist me."

During the course of that day, Bridget quickly became accustomed to answering to the name Bertie. Margaret used it often.

"Bertie, get the lace trim from that drawer."

"Hand me those shears, Bertie."

"Bertie, cut along these lines."

Bertie Miller. It had a nice, modern, American sound to it. New country. New life. New name. She might enjoy being Bertie Miller, she decided.

She was relieved that the stern Margaret apparently had not believed any of Paddy's false claims about her sewing ability. Margaret left Bridget, now Bertie, to do the mundane tasks of cutting pattern lines she expertly chalked onto the fabric. She had her do the pinning and the cutting, keeping the more complex aspects of the job for herself.

By five o'clock, the largest of the female dummies wore a gorgeous green brocade dress with velvet trim of dark chocolate brown, with a lace collar edged in tiny pearls. In the back of the gown was the same kind of flounce she had observed on the women in the park on the day they'd seen the gigantic hand with the torch. "Do these women truly have such large rears?" she asked, fingering the extra fabric in back.

Margaret looked at her in surprise, but then the smallest flicker of a smile crossed her thin lips. "A bustle goes in there."

"Pardon?"

"It's a kind of basketlike structure that gives the dress its fashionable shape."

"Well, that's a relief, ma'am," Bridget, newly Bertie, said. "I thought the poor things must be truly misshapen."

"You didn't," Margaret gasped.

"Well, it was hard to believe, but I couldn't figure any other reason for such a shape," she admitted.

Margaret studied her a moment. "I believe you will be learning a lot here, Bertie. Clean the scraps and toss them in the bin over there. Put the extra fabric into that paper bag over there."

"Yes, ma'am."

While Bertie tidied, Margaret took out a pad and swiftly sketched the dress and wrote some measurements on the paper, also an address. "Bertie, I'm sending you to the milliner's shop."

The what? "Pardon?" she inquired.

"The hatmaker," Margaret explained. "This hat-maker's shop is east of here at this address on Fourteenth Street. Give them the material and trim on that table. Tell them I want a hat of the latest fashion suitable for making calls in the afternoon to go with this dress. Ask them to adorn it with feathers, preferably from a pheasant, and to spare no expense. Make sure to find out how soon they can have it ready. I don't show Miss Elizabeth anything until all the parts have been completed."

"Yes, ma'am. I'll be happy to," Bertie agreed, smiling. She couldn't believe she was being entrusted to leave the building and go out on her own on her very first day. She had never seen a hatmaker's shop and was excited to embark on the adventure.

"Don't get too excited," warned Margaret. "I expect you to return promptly."

"Understood, ma'am," Bertie assured her. "I'll be quick about it."

"See that you are," Margaret said.

In minutes Bertie was scurrying down the stairs, carrying a brocade bag full of the material. She was on the staircase, nearly to the bottom floor, when the front door opened and the hallway exploded with the sound of raucous male laughter.

Two young men in their late teens stepped inside. The first one in was tall and broad-shouldered. Thick blond hair curled over the top of his opened white shirt collar. From the fact that his form so closely matched that of his dressmaker's model in the sewing room, she assumed he must be the junior Mr. Wellington.

His chortling companion was shorter and heavier, with tight curls cut close to his head. He had kept his jacket on but loosened his tie and collar. The two of them were engaged in the discussion of something that obviously caused them great amusement.

As Bertie came toward them, they noticed her. "Hello. Judging from your smock, I'm guessing you're the new sewing girl?" Mr. Wellington Jr. inquired.

"Yes, sir." She had never seen a fellow so good-looking. He was indeed like a prince from a story, though instead of a doublet and cape he wore a crisp white shirt and slung a town coat over his shoulder.

"Please! Don't call me sir! You can call me Master Wellington when my father or anyone else is around, and James when we're alone. And what is your name?"

"Bertie Miller."

"I like it. What a modern name. My friend here is George Rumpole, a former classmate at the illustrious St. Paul's Academy, where we went to school until just barely graduating last June."

"Congratulations," said Bertie.

"No congratulations warranted, you can be sure," said George Rumpole. "James was last and I was second to last in our esteemed class."

"Not for lack of brains, though," James insisted.

"No, not at all," agreed George. "It was merely for lack of expending any effort whatsoever."

"Absolutely right," James said proudly. "We graduated, did we not? And we had a blazing good time while getting to that point. I believe we *should* be congratulated for accomplishing our goal while economizing on effort and preserving our precious time so that it could be spent in the pursuit of far more entertaining endeavors."

"Well done, then," Bertie said. These two were a lot of fun, and though they might be scalawags, they made her smile.

"See? This girl understands what's important," James praised her. "Listen, Bertie Miller, there are some shirts on the chair in my room that are in need of buttons. Could you go in later and get them?"

"Yes, sir."

"James."

"James."

That evening Bertie left her smock up in her quarters and went home wearing her plain blue dress. She knew she should have changed to keep it clean, but she couldn't bear to take it off. As she made her way downtown through the increasingly noisy, odorous, dirty streets, she lifted her hem as high as she dared to avoid the filth from the streets.

As she went, her mind swam with all the new terms and techniques she'd learned from Margaret. She could hardly believe the skill and speed with which the woman had cut out and sewn up the exquisite gown.

Her journey to the milliner had taken her through the garment district, where she had seen shops of every kind specializing in all aspects of clothing manufacture. She'd seen shops dedicated exclusively to ribbon, lace, and many kinds of trimming, and some that displayed only one thing: a seemingly infinite variety of buttons of all descriptions. She'd seen large factories and small shops set side by side.

The shop where she had been sent was narrow and wedged between two much larger establishments. On the front glass, etched in swirling calligraphy, was the name: LADIES' HATS OF PARIS.

Inside were two fashionably dressed ladies, whom she guessed, based on their resemblance to each other, to be sisters. The younger one smiled at her cordially when she came in. "*Bonjour, mademoiselle.* How can I help you this day?" she said in a French accent Bertie found musical and completely charming.

The same younger sister studied the picture of the dress and examined the fabrics. "Madame Margaret is a genius! I can design a *chapeau très joli* to set off this dress. I know just the thing."

Now, as Bertie approached her block, filled with peeled paint, dull browns and grays, and all the earmarks of dire poverty, she thought of these things: J. P. Wellington's fine home, the gorgeous hat shop, even her neat, lavender-scented room on the servants' floor. She hated to leave it all.

A fierce longing welled up inside her. How could

she get a life like this? It didn't have to be a house like the Wellingtons owned. But to own a shop like the sisters from Paris—that seemed like paradise, and it wasn't such an impossible dream, was it?

She would watch Margaret closely, learn from her. She would acquire every skill that she could. Bertie stopped and leaned against a building, shutting her eyes to bring her little shop into focus in her mind. She saw her name engraved on a front window in the same fine hand as that on the hat shop: BERTIE MILLER'S FINE AMERICAN DRESSES. Using her new name would instantly announce that her shop would be modern and chic. Bridget O'Malley's Dress Shop didn't sound nearly as fashionable.

Her eyes opened and she hurried on. As she left, James Wellington came into her head.

You can call me James when we're alone.

A guilty shiver ran through her. Did he intend for them to be alone? It would be so lovely to be alone with him, to have his handsome, lively eyes focused only on her.

That afternoon she'd picked up the shirts from his chair, and before bringing them in to Margaret, she'd lifted them to her face and smelled them. She'd inhaled the heady scent of woodsy cologne, and it had stayed with her. She could call it up even now.

She stopped for a chicken thigh and a carrot on the way home. She added three potatoes to her bag, feeling that she could afford to spend all she had on a decent meal. With her groceries under her arm, she climbed the stairs to her building and was met by Liam on the top landing.

"What is it?" she asked urgently, instantly reading the worried look on his face.

"It's Eileen. Something is wrong with her," he said.

CHAPTER NINE
Crisis

That night Bertie sat on the fire escape with Eileen in her lap, mopping the little girl's feverish brow with a damp cloth. It was ironic, she thought; she now had enough money to feed the child properly, but Eileen couldn't eat. Her throat was red and swollen. The glands under her fragile chin were like two eggs. At intervals, she hacked out a barking cough that seemed to rattle her small frame.

A young woman appeared at the window—Maria from Mrs. Howard's sweatshop. "I came by to visit you, and your brother told me you have a sick *bambina*," she explained, climbing out onto the escape.

"It's true. I don't know what to do for her," Bertie said fretfully. "I'm glad to see you, anyway. Are you still with Mrs. Howard?"

"No. I got a better job. Now I'm making pasta in the kitchen of a tavern. You ever heard of spaghetti?"

Bertie shook her head and chuckled. "I don't think I could even say it."

"You'll love it. I'll bring you some with tomato sauce."

"Potato sauce?"

"Tomato sauce! Haven't you ever had a tomato?"

"Never," Bertie admitted.

"Oh, this is a strange city that has people who never ate tomatoes!" exclaimed Maria. "My mother grows them on our fire escape. I'll bring you one, Bridget."

"It's Bertie now—I've gone American," she told Maria, and then filled her in on her new job at J. P. Wellington's. She was just about to mention the good-looking James Wellington when Eileen interrupted them with another fit of coughing.

"I hope it's not the diphtheria," Maria commented, frowning with worry.

"The what?" asked Bertie, alarmed.

"Has she got a sore throat?"

"Terrible sore, and swollen."

Maria felt the girl's swollen glands and nodded seriously. "It could be. Is her throat red or is it all filmy white?"

"Red."

"That's good. If it gets the film over it, it could be diphtheria. A bunch of children in my building had it."

"How long did it take for them to get well?"

A guarded expression appeared on Maria's face.

"Tell me what happened to them," Bertie insisted.

"Two of them seem to be getting better," said Maria, not meeting Bertie's eyes.

"And the others?" Bertie pressed.

Maria shook her head.

"They're not improving?"

"You'd better get her to a doctor," Maria said.

"What happened to those children?" Bertie demanded.

"They didn't make it," Maria murmured.

Bertie left Eileen in Liam's care in the morning, not knowing what else to do. "Maybe it's just a bug of some kind," she said hopefully. "Keep wiping her all over with a damp cloth—that will keep the fever down. There's chicken broth on the stove. It's full of healthy things for a sick person. See if you can feed her some. We can't let her get too weak."

"I don't feel so good, Bridget," Liam complained.

She felt his forehead and shook her head. "I don't feel a fever. Be strong, Liam. If you get sick now, what will I do? Try to stay healthy."

"How do I do that?"

"I'm sure I don't know. Try your best."

She arrived at the townhouse, panting from running the last several blocks, fearful of being late. She ran from the kitchen up to her room on the top floor and threw on her smock. She heard the grandfather clock in the front hall gong seven as she entered the sewing room.

"Were you out carousing last night?" asked Margaret, who was already seated behind the sewing machine.

"Pardon, ma'am?"

"You have circles under your eyes, you're pale, and your hair is a mess."

Bertie clutched the red curls that she'd thrown into a quick bun at home and realized they'd come mostly undone in her dash uptown. "Sorry, ma'am. It was a hard night because my little sister was taken with some kind of ailment and we didn't sleep much."

"What kind of ailment?"

"I'm not sure. My friend thought it might be dip-something."

The look of horror that ran across Margaret's face made Bertie wish she could pull her words back out of the air.

"Bertie," said Margaret, "if your sister comes down with diphtheria, you are to inform me at once. We cannot have this household infected. Is that understood?"

"Yes ma'am." All Bertie truly understood was that she would say no more about Eileen's sickness, and if asked, she would claim that the girl was better.

Margaret kept her busy with sewing chores all day, she didn't have a moment to find Paddy or Seamus in the carriage house. At six, when she was dismissed, she went to look for them. "Da has gone to pick up Mr. Wellington at some ferry or boat or something," Seamus told her excitedly. "I think it's pretty far away."

"Tell him I need money for a doctor for Eileen," she said.

"I don't think he has any," said Seamus.

"What do you mean he has none? He's working, isn't he?"

"He went out with Mike O'Fallon last night and paid him back the money he owed him. He said he's tapped out until next payday. Don't you have any?"

"I spent what I had on food before I knew Eileen was sick. Maybe she'll be improved when I get home."

But that night a thick film formed over Eileen's throat and tongue, as Maria had predicted it might. The little girl wheezed and coughed. "She can't breathe!" Bertie realized, scooping the child into a blanket and heading out the door with her, not sure where she was going.

She hit the street, wondering what to do.

Ray Stalls was leaning against a building across the street, talking with another man. When he saw her, he crossed. "What's the matter?"

"She can't breathe!"

"Come on, follow me." She ran behind him through the crowded street, racing down alleyways that led to other alleys. They hurried between two buildings where drunks weaved in front of them and a thuggish man stood with a shotgun. She had no time to worry about them. Eileen was wheezing harder and turning paler by the moment. "Come on. You're too slow. Hurry," he urged her over his shoulder.

Then he stopped and took Eileen from her. "Go up these stairs," he said, directing Bertie into a dark building and down a narrow hallway. When he reached the top, he yanked open a door and they hurried into a crowded waiting room. "Tell Dr. Umberto that it's an emergency," he told the nurse.

The nurse, a short, dark-haired Italian woman, looked at the child in his arms and disappeared into an inner office. In a second she waved them in.

Dr. Umberto was short and bald. The sleeves of his white shirt were pushed up to his elbows. "How long she like this?" he asked in a heavy Italian accent.

"Since yesterday," Bertie reported.

The doctor laid Eileen on a table and took a narrow tube from a case. Prying her small mouth open, he fed it down the child's throat. Eileen began to sputter and wheeze. "She'll choke," Bertie objected.

"She no choke," Dr. Umberto stated, without looking away from Eileen.

"It's called an intubation," Ray told her. "I've seen it done before. They used to cut the throat open. This is much better."

The doctor nodded. "It's true."

Eileen's chest began to rise and fall more steadily. The nurse wiped the sweat from her face. "You should leave her here until her condition stabilizes," she said with only the hint of an accent. "Come back in an hour."

"I have no money!" Bertie blurted without thinking.

"I have money," said Ray. "I can cover it."

"It is good thing you bring her in," Dr. Umberto said. "You just make it in time."

A cracked, anguished gasp shot from Bertie's lips. What was he saying?

Would Eileen have died?

She clapped her hand over her mouth, nauseated at the thought of it. Afraid that she would vomit right there, she lunged out of the office through the busy waiting room and into the dark hall. Leaning against its wall, she put her arm up and panted. The still coolness of the hallway slowly settled her lurching stomach, and her breath slowed. Ray stood beside her silently.

Turning, she fell on his shoulder, sobbing. "I can never thank you enough. Never."

CHAPTER TEN
James Wellington, The Prince of Industry

Three days later Bertie stepped beside Margaret to watch Elizabeth Wellington turn in the mirror of the sewing room. She was about twenty, pretty and petite, with a head of meticulously coiffed, upswept hair. The young woman was trying on the green brocade dress with the brown velvet trim and its matching hat.

The Parisian sisters had fashioned a tall bonnet festooned with brown netting and an abundance of some poor pheasant's iridescently shimmering brown, green, and black feathers elaborately interwoven with brown velvet cord. Bertie thought the hat was gorgeous beyond any words she had to describe it.

"Can you take it in a little in the middle?" Elizabeth requested, pouting fretfully at her image. "My waist is tiny, and I want to show it off. The hourglass shape is so popular this season."

"Certainly, miss," replied Margaret. Bertie found it odd, even a bit unsettling, to see the imperious Margaret so subservient.

"And this hat . . ." Elizabeth squinted and cocked her head to the side critically. "I'm not sure about it. What do you think?"

"It's like a dream," Bertie offered. Margaret glanced at her sharply, and Bertie realized she had spoken out of place.

Bertie lowered her eyes and went back to her own private thoughts. She was just as happy not to be involved. She was tired from staying up half the night, watching over Eileen, making sure her small chest was rising and falling evenly as she slept.

Bertie worried constantly that Liam wouldn't be up to the challenge of caring for a sick little girl. Luckily, Finn's hours had been cut back at the firehouse. Even though it meant he was making less salary, at least he was able to come home earlier to relieve Liam of caring for Eileen.

"You're new here, aren't you?" Elizabeth said directly to Bertie, jolting her from her worried thoughts about Eileen.

"This is Bertie Miller," Margaret introduced her, "the daughter of your new carriage driver. She's my assistant."

"Oh, you're the one my brother told me about," Elizabeth said with an air of excitement. "I think he's a little taken with you. He said how pretty you are." She stepped back and regarded Bertie. "You know, you *are* pretty, at that. I'd kill to have your hair."

Bertie dropped her eyes down and flushed with embarrassment, flattered nonetheless. "Thank you, miss."

Two more young women entered the room, holding some dresses in their arms: one a thinner, taller, yet younger version of Miss Elizabeth; the other a rounder, rosier, and still younger edition of the other two. Elizabeth introduced Bertie to them. "These are my sisters, Catherine and Alice."

"Are you the girl from Wales?" asked Alice, the youngest.

"Don't be daft, she's obviously Irish," said Catherine.

Bertie's heart jumped a beat. Was her father's lie so obvious? If J. P. Wellington knew they were Irish, would he fire them? "Are you Irish?" Alice asked boldly.

"Of course she is," Catherine insisted. "Look at that hair! That's Irish hair. I'd adore having dangerous red hair."

"Dangerous, miss?" Bertie questioned.

"Oh, yes," stated Catherine emphatically. "Redheaded women are glamorous and hotheaded, even a little crazy."

Bertie thought of her fantasy about being a princess. Maybe she was, indeed, slightly crazy. "Why would a person want to be crazy?" she dared to ask.

"Because it's daring and romantic," Catherine

replied. "In *Jane Eyre*, Mr. Rochester has a crazy wife locked in the attic. Have you read the novel? It was written nearly forty years ago, but it still seems modern today."

"No, I haven't, miss." At that moment nothing on earth could have compelled Bertie to admit she'd never learned to read. These young women lived in such a different world. What she wouldn't give to be part of it.

"But you haven't answered me," Alice kept on insistently. "Are you Irish? It won't matter. We had one great-grandmother from the north of Ireland."

"Young ladies, Bertie needs to help me make some alterations on Miss Elizabeth's new outfit," Margaret cut in, relieving Bertie of the obligation to answer. "Forgive me for taking her from you. Is there something you would like me to do in regard to the dresses you are holding?"

"Yes," Alice told Margaret, handing the dresses off to Bertie. "They're from last fall. Would you donate these to the mission for us as you always do? Some poor girl might as well have the benefit of them."

"That's most charitable," Margaret commended. "Let me know when you will be available to be fitted for new dresses."

"We will," Catherine promised. "Father is downstairs, and he just brought home this season's pattern books from his factory."

"When did your father arrive?" asked Margaret.

"Last night," Elizabeth told her as she took off her

hat. "His new coachman made excellent time traveling up the Jersey shoreline. He says that he rode like a madman, which he half suspects he is." She glanced at Bertie and smiled, covering her mouth as if embarrassed at having spoken without thinking. "That's your father, isn't it? No offense intended."

"Yes, miss, none taken." Bertie wasn't sure if the offense had been intentional or not. Her father did seem half-mad even to her sometimes, overzealous if always well-intentioned, and she could see how someone might take him for a lunatic upon first meeting.

"We'll be deciding on our new dresses once we look through the pattern books," Catherine added. "That's why we're clearing out these old dresses to make room for the new."

"In that case we shall be quite busy and must get to work," Margaret declared.

Catherine and Alice stayed to watch, draping themselves along the arms and back of the one cushioned chair, while Elizabeth modeled her new outfit, wearing it inside out so Margaret could make the requested alteration.

"I have some old dresses from last year to give you as well," Elizabeth said, as Margaret nipped in the dress waist with the pins Bertie handed her from the little cushion she held.

"But you know, Margaret, before you donate those dresses, you should offer them to the servant girls. I'm sure some of them would be happy to have them."

"The servants don't want our old cast-off things,"

Alice jumped in, with a glance at Bertie. "You don't want those old dresses, do you, Bertie? I'm sure you have your own dresses that are perfectly fine."

Pride nearly made Bertie agree that she had no need for anyone's old clothing. The words had already formed and were just waiting to be set free, when her eyes fell upon the dresses, which now sat in a pile on one of the cutting tables. They looked as though they had never been worn!

How could she turn down such a gift?

Her mother had always said that false pride was a sin—and in this case, it would have been utter foolishness—so she swallowed her self-important words. "I would love some of those dresses," she admitted.

"They wouldn't fit you," Catherine observed.

"I'm a seamstress," Bertie reminded her. "Miss Alice is shorter than I am, but I could take that deep blue dress and remove the skirt of the ruffled yellow to use as an underskirt to lengthen it. Then I could detach the sleeves and add a yellow ruffle to the blue."

"You are a natural stylist, I see," Margaret commented, sounding genuinely impressed.

"My mother taught me to work with what I had," she replied, recalling how her mother had never wasted anything, not even the buttons from torn or worn-out garments.

"Take the whole batch of them, then," said Catherine. "The other servant girls are probably too heavy to fit them anyway."

"Thank you. You are very generous," Bertie replied, as she looked to Margaret to see if it was indeed all right for her to accept the gift. Margaret nodded almost imperceptibly, and Bertie's spirits soared, thrilled by this newfound wealth.

At six o'clock Bertie carried the pile of dresses up into her small maid's room and tossed them lightly onto the bed, eager to examine them more closely. She sat down hard on the end of the bed, blowing some hair from her eyes.

It had been a long day, with hardly any time to even eat anything. Margaret had explained to her that when Mr. Wellington arrived from his mills with the new pattern books from Europe, it was the busiest time of the year. The Wellington girls scoured the catalogs, wanting every latest fashion. "You'd better be prepared to put in some long days from now until Christmas," she warned Bertie. "September is half over now, and Miss Catherine will be making her debut in society in early November. After Thanksgiving there will be holiday parties and balls for them all. Each event requires a new frock. Even young Mr. Wellington will require several new outfits, though now that he's graduated, his father will no doubt start having his suits tailored in London."

She picked up a taffeta dress with blue and green stripes that had belonged to Catherine. The dress's full, shiny taffeta skirt was intricately pleated at the boned waist and swished deliciously as she held it in front of her. The other sisters were shorter than she, but Catherine was the closest to her size, and her things would be the easiest to alter.

Where she would ever wear such a rich-looking gown as this she had no idea, but it was a joy just to own it.

Spreading all the dresses out on the narrow bed, she allowed herself another minute to select one or two to bring back to the apartment to alter to her size in the evening. It had sadly occurred to her that there were other uses for the dresses than to keep them as gowns. They could be torn at the seams and their fabric used to make shirts and vests for her brothers and father, and she promised herself to make some blouses and smock dresses for Eileen.

She sat on the edge of the bed, thinking about Eileen. Though she'd seemed to improve quickly after coming home from the doctor's office, Eileen was still sick. Her fever had gone down, but the cough and filmy throat persisted. All she could muster the energy to do was loll on the mattress playing with her rag doll. Yes, one of these gowns would make several cute dresses for Eileen. And there was one that was a little looser fitting than the others; it might look good on Maria. Tonight when she came by to visit—which she did almost every evening lately—Bertie would offer it to her, and they could make any alterations that were needed.

She was staring at the dresses and thinking of

what to make for Eileen when her door burst open. Looking up in surprise, she gasped to see young James Wellington standing in the small room, facing her.

"Sir?" she asked, startled.

"James," he reminded her. "We're alone."

You can call me James when we're alone.

She was very aware that they were alone—and standing quite close together, since the room was no more than a large closet. Up close, he was even more handsome than she had recalled. "Can I help you? I mean, why are you here?"

"My cursed father!" he said angrily. "Things are so nice when he's away, but he always returns!"

"I'm sorry, but I don't understand."

"I'm hiding! Don't you see? This is the last place he would look for me. What are you doing here? Hiding from Margaret, I don't doubt."

"This is my room," she told him.

He blinked, not understanding. "You're not living here, are you?"

"It's a sort of changing room—a courtesy, I imagine. It comes with the position."

"Oh. Well, I am sorry, then. I didn't realize." He looked her up and down with a direct gaze. "Nice to run into you again, at any rate. You know, you're even prettier than I remembered, and I recalled you as being very pretty indeed."

He smiled, and she returned the smile despite her concerns about the impropriety of this situation.

"Why are you hiding from your father?" she asked.

"Blast him! He is so unreasonable. My illustrious father just discovered that I have been rejected from Harvard. Up until this moment I don't think he was fully aware of exactly how badly I did at St. Paul's Academy. I tried to explain to him that it was no matter because I don't even want to go to Harvard— or any university, for that matter. I want to join him in running the family textile mills. I'm his son. I'm old enough now."

"And he doesn't want you to work with him?" asked Bertie.

"No! He wants me to be a lawyer or the president of the United States or some other dull thing like that. But I'm built for business. I like making money, or rather, directing others to make it for me. Besides, I have no interest in academics."

"And he's very angry at you?" she asked.

"He's in a towering rage," he replied. "I stormed out of his study, but I couldn't think of anywhere to go that he wouldn't find me, except here. Mind if I wait with you here until the coast is clear?"

"I don't think it's quite proper. I could be fired."

"I won't let them fire you."

"I have my reputation to think of."

He smiled at her wolfishly.

She knew she should be worried, even offended, but she found him so charming. "You can stay a few more minutes, and then you must go. Please," she said.

"Thank you," he said, taking her hand.

She knew she should pull it away, but his hand was large and strong. Her rough, work-worn palm felt delicate when he held it.

He lifted her hand to his lips and bent his head to it, placing a long, warm kiss just above her knuckles. Then, raising his head slightly, he gazed into her eyes. "You have saved me," he said, without a trace of mockery. "I am in your debt."

CHAPTER ELEVEN
The Secret Room

The image of James Wellington took up permanent residence inside Bertie's head. She forced herself to wash the hand he had kissed but found it consoling to think that he had left an indelible if invisible mark there that no amount of scrubbing could ever remove.

She didn't daydream about marrying him in a grand ceremony or even of eloping with him on the sly. No future together would be possible for them— he was a prince of industry, the heir apparent, sure to inherit his father's company and wealth. They lived in different worlds that would never meet—so she did not imagine a future with him.

He was simply there in her mind every second that some task did not divert her from thinking of him. She was helpless to control it, even if she had wanted to. And part of her very much wanted to stop thinking of him. It made her feel like a silly girl, this unbridled, senseless mooning over a handsome, educated, gentleman son of a millionaire whom she could never make her own.

It was ridiculous!

But there it was, just the same. She could find no way to make it stop.

So she spent the next week learning the fine points of making tissue-paper patterns, cutting, pinning, and sewing them with greater refinement than she had known even existed. Margaret began teaching her to use a sewing machine, a thing she relished learning and took to quickly.

The parts of her mind not bent on learning what Margaret had to teach were spent worrying about Eileen, who was still coughing and weak.

Finn had now been laid off from the firehouse entirely. "Last hired, first fired," he explained. "They're cutting the number of firehouses, supposedly to save taxpayers money." The good news was that he was able to stay home with Eileen and took adequate care of her. At least, that's what Bertie had thought at first, but in actuality he spent most of his days poring through the newspapers in search of a new job and in teaching Liam to read and write. Bertie worried that Eileen was not getting the attention she needed. Sometimes when she came home in the evening, the little girl seemed listless and the place was a mess.

At home in the evenings, Bertie ripped out the seams of most of the cast-off dresses and refashioned them into vests, shirts, and underwear for her father and the boys. She used one of them to make Eileen's smocks and saved the three gowns she liked best for herself. The remaining gowns she used to make extra bows and trim to add to the other three in order to make them fit. With her new sewing skills, she was gratified to see that the workmanship in these garments was better than anything she had ever previously produced.

And all the while she was doing these things, like a subterranean spring running below all her surface thoughts, James Wellington was there: his handsome face, his wolfish grin, his shining, mirthful eyes, and his woodsy cologne. The picture she savored most strongly consisted of no more than the memory of a fleeting moment, the swiftest glance. The moment had come just as he was leaving her room. He had turned to say good-bye, and their eyes had met. She saw then how attracted he was to her.

It had taken her breath away to think that he—so handsome, so desirable—could be attracted to her.

When Saturday morning finally arrived, Finn went out to talk to a friend and came back elated. "They have a spot for me in a firehouse in Boston," he announced. "I have to leave right away."

"That's great, Finn," she said. Neither of them was sure where Boston was, but Finn would be traveling with his friend.

"I'm sorry to leave you here with the kids. How much longer will you be staying in the apartment?"

"I'm going to try to keep it going. Da wants me to give it up, but the Wellingtons won't want Eileen and Liam living in the carriage house, and my room is too small."

"I could take Liam with me, but then who would watch Eileen?"

"I don't know," she said. "It's not fair to Liam, though. He should be in school."

Finn shrugged. "I've taught him some of what I know."

"I envy him that," Bertie admitted. "Someday maybe you'll teach me to read. Or maybe Liam will."

A silence fell between them for a moment. "I hate to see you go," she said, breaking it.

"I know," he said. "I hate leaving you here to deal with everything. There's a lot on you these days. I know that, even if Da doesn't."

Emotional tears jumped unexpectedly into the corners of her eyes. It made her happy that he saw all she was doing. She didn't expect praise, but his appreciative words touched her just the same. She wrapped him in a hug, squeezing tight. "I'll miss you," she said.

"We'll be together again," he replied, a catch in his throat as he held on to her another moment.

Finn left late that night. After saying good-bye to him, she went to bed and lay listening to Eileen's heavy wheeze. Had this illness left the child permanently frail? As Eileen slept in the moonlight, her porcelain skin seemed nearly transparent, with lines of blue veins at her temples. The illness had turned her into a whisper of her former self.

In the morning Bertie rose early and got a bucket of water from the hall sink. She washed her hair with the same bar of soap she used for the dishes, sticking her head out the window and rinsing it by pouring the water over her head.

Toweling her hair dry, she put on one of the second-hand dresses, the blue and green striped. It would take too long to wait for the mass of curls to dry, so she twisted it into a knot, pinning it into place.

Today she would go to church and pray for Eileen. It was the only thing she could think of to do. She would be back before Eileen and Liam even awoke.

She knew where to find the church, because she passed it each day on her walk uptown. Although it was only a neighborhood church, it was higher and grander than any she'd known back in Ireland.

Bertie found it comforting to hear the words of the Mass spoken in Latin. It was a language she did not understand, but the sounds were familiar from her childhood, when she'd attended Mass every Sunday. All the while she kept her thoughts on Eileen, begging God and his mother, Mary, to help her get better. Once or twice James Wellington came unbidden into her mind, but he was quickly banished.

After Mass she placed a penny in the tin collection box to light a candle for Eileen and knelt to say one more prayer. By the time she was done, most of the others had left the church. She went out of the dark, cool, silent building and once more returned to the bustle of the street.

She was heading toward home when Ray Stalls fell into step with her. "You are looking quite the lady today," he complimented her.

Since the day he had gotten Eileen to the doctor, she had dropped her wary suspicion of him. How could she be anything but cordial to him after all he'd done for her and her family? "Thank you," she said.

"How is the little girl?" he asked. That night, in the hallway outside the doctor's office, after she had finished crying on his shoulder, he had excused himself, saying he had an appointment he could not miss. She had not seen him since.

"She is better but not much," Bertie reported. "I'm worried about her."

"So many little children get sick," he commented sympathetically. "Children cannot stay healthy in these filthy conditions, without proper water or food."

"She wouldn't be as healthy as she is if you hadn't helped us," she declared.

"Ach!" he said, waving his hand dismissively.

"You know, we have never been introduced," she pointed out.

"My name is Ray Stalls," he said, extending his hand to shake.

"Mine is Bertie Miller," she replied, shaking.

"Is that your real name?" they both asked at the same time, their voices overlapping.

"It depends what you mean by real," Ray considered. "Here, in America, this is really my name. Is it the name I was born with? No."

"The same for me," she admitted. "What is your real name?"

"It's a secret."

"I was born Bridget O'Malley," she offered.

"That is a lovely name, as is Bertie Miller. My real name is not as lovely, and so I will keep it to myself."

"That's not fair," she argued.

"Nothing is fair."

"But America is the land of equality for all, is it not?" she stated.

"It is a lofty goal, yes. It is certainly better than the places we came from, where no one even thinks equality is something to strive for."

"But you don't think everyone is equal?" she questioned.

"Does it look like that is true to you?" he countered.

She thought of life at the Wellington home and her life in her Five Points tenement. Clearly they were not equal. "Everyone is equal in the eyes of God," she remarked.

He smiled. "All right. Maybe there."

She stopped at a narrow building, where wire chicken coops were stacked atop one another and hens laid eggs that went instantly on sale. She wanted to buy three for breakfast. Ray took out a leather wallet. "Can I help?" he offered.

Bertie waved him off. "You've already helped more than I can repay. What do you do that you always have so much money?"

He grinned. "I'm a burglar, remember?"

"I'm sorry I said that."

"You are forgiven. I am a tailor by day, and by night I am excellent at cards and so increase my day's wage."

"Aren't you afraid you'll *lose* your day's wage instead?" she asked, taking the paper bag of eggs from the vendor.

"Not meaning to boast, but . . . I never lose."

She laughed at his bravado. "Is that so?"

"It's true," he confirmed.

"And how did you learn to be a tailor?" she asked, continuing to walk on toward home.

A distant look swept across his face for a moment before he spoke. "It is a long and pitiful story," he said with a bitter laugh. "Are you sure you want to hear it?"

"I'm sure."

He told her that as a young boy of about seven he had been sold to a traveling carnival show by his parents, who were so poor that they could not feed him. At the carnival he had worked as an acrobat, a juggler, and a tightrope walker.

"That's why you can swing around on the fire escape like that," she realized.

He nodded. "We traveled all through Europe and Russia. I worked with a magician, too. I know lots of magic. I became better than the magician I assisted, so one night he knocked me out and left me behind on the side of the road. It was in Moscow, I think. I was nine."

"How terrible," she said with a gasp. "What did you do?"

"The only thing I could," he replied. "I stood on corners and juggled and walked on my hands and flipped in the air for what coins people would throw at me. Those coins were enough for me to buy a piece of bread and sometimes a blanket so I wouldn't freeze to death on the park benches where I slept."

"How did you get to America?"

"I stowed away on a steamer. I was doing my usual tricks in the park—"

"The one with the torch?" she interrupted.

"Yes, but the torch wasn't there then. I was dirty and raggedy and not too many people wanted to stop to see me in that condition, so I wasn't doing too well. Then, one day, a tailor who I had seen watching me for about a week came along and took my by the filthy shirt collar and said, 'You will work with me. I will teach you to be a tailor.'"

"He adopted you, then?"

"Yes and no. His wife cleaned me up and fed me. But I lived and worked in the shop. It was my whole life. A funny thing happened too. As I learned, I began to remember my life as a child when I was very young. I recalled things that I had forgotten, such as that my grandmother was a spinner and I would help her spin the wool in a barn behind where we once lived. And I remembered my parents sewing inside our small home."

"And now you are a tailor," she said.

"Yes, it was as though I was meant to be in the garment trade, and no amount of strange turns on life's path could change that fact."

"Life is strange," Bertie remarked.

"It is, indeed," he agreed thoughtfully.

"Do you still live at the tailor shop?"

"No, that shop closed when the man died, and I worked for several other tailors after that. I was back on the street again, but this time I at least had money in my pocket; plus, I was older by then and it became easier to make my own way."

She observed him more closely than she ever had before and saw why she'd previously found his age so hard to judge. She saw now that he was probably younger than twenty, not much older than herself, but all that he'd been through had left a hardness, more like a deep weariness, in and around his dark eyes. Maybe it was just sadness.

His face lit with a thought, and he suddenly appeared to be as young as he really was. "Do you want to see something I just found?"

"What?" she asked, thinking that he was really quite pleasant-looking when he smiled. Until this moment she had not seen him smile with anything other than bitter irony. His smile of real pleasure— appearing so unexpectedly, like the sun suddenly rising from behind a cloud—raised an answering smile from her.

"Come with me." He picked up his pace, and impulsively she followed him. In two blocks he turned down an empty alley, where he lifted the hatch of a basement cellar and climbed down. Bertie went down after him.

It was cold and dark, but the open door above provided enough light to reveal an abandoned room. At its center sat a broken spinning wheel.

"When is the last time you saw one of those?" he asked happily, excitement animating his face.

In truth, it hadn't been that long ago. Her mother had had an old spinning wheel like this one, which she had used to spin the fleece from their one sheep until they had to sell the animal. Her mother had once shown her how to use it, but she'd forgotten now.

"And look at this," he added, directing her attention to a small hand loom. "All this is done in big textile mills now. Someone must have had a little home shop down here once."

"What's upstairs?" she asked. "These things must belong to someone."

"I don't know. The building is boarded up. I broke in just the other night looking for a place to sleep. Remember that very hot night? I came down here thinking it would be cooler, and I found these."

"Why don't you get a regular place to live?" she asked him. He seemed to have enough money.

"I haven't had a home since I was seven. The idea of it makes me nervous. I'm happier flopping down anywhere that's convenient." He looked away from her as if wanting to change the subject. "Isn't this hand loom great? I want to clean it up and see if I can use it."

"Would you make cloth?" she asked.

"I don't know yet. I just want to see what I can do with them."

He stepped closer to her—too close, she thought, but for some reason she didn't move away. "You are very pretty in that new dress, you know, princess," he said, his voice dropping to the thick, unmistakable tones of attraction.

"Why do you call me princess?" she asked him, no longer content to let it hang as a mystery between them.

"Because I can see you as you really are."

"How can you?"

"When you grow up on the streets, you learn to see into people. You need to if you are to survive. I can see beyond the ragged skirt and even this cast-off dress to the royal blood that courses through your veins."

She felt laid bare, exposed; her deepest secret revealed. And yet he had said it. She had not claimed to be any princess. He had claimed it for her.

He knew what she knew, what she felt deep down. But how?

He looked her over and then took her hand.

"Come on. Let's get out of here. People will talk if they find us down here together, and you don't need that."

"What will they say?" she asked as she climbed the stairs ahead of him, wanting to hear his version of what she knew the gossip would be.

"They will ask why the beautiful red-haired princess from Ireland lowered herself to consort with that no-good gambling troll of a tailor from who knows where."

CHAPTER TWELVE
Da's Wild Boast

Over the next two weeks, it became clear that Paddy O'Malley, now Rick Miller, had not been wrong when he boasted of his daughter's skills, even though she had not yet acquired those skills at the time of his boast. Under the expert tutelage of Margaret, Bertie soared to new heights of dressmaking, even daring to design her own dresses based on the patterns she saw in J. P. Wellington's thick books and to create tissue-paper patterns of her own.

And Bertie adored the work. She discovered dexterity in her hands that she had never realized she possessed, since she hadn't ever had the chance to do such fine, delicate work before. She folded in pleats and finished buttonholes with such skill that even the exacting Margaret was impressed. Her attention to detail was top-notch, and soon Margaret trusted her to put in collars of the most expensive lace.

The early October nights became chilly, relieving the blistering heat of an Indian summer that had dogged the city dwellers all the way through September. It made life in her tenement somewhat more bearable.

Eileen improved, but she continued to wheeze and cough. Bertie wanted to bring her sister back to Dr. Umberto, but her paycheck just covered their needs. Her father gave her money each week, but all it did was allow her to hold on to the apartment.

She was reconsidering Paddy's idea for Mike O'Fallon's sister to take Eileen and let Liam go live with Finn in Boston, but she couldn't stand the thought of her family being broken up like that.

She thought of asking Maria to look in on them during her breaks from the restaurant where she now worked, but worried that it was too big a favor.

From time to time she ran into Ray on the street and always felt a mixture of gladness and uneasiness. He continued to simply pop up unannounced and uninvited in the oddest places, as though he had some sort of ability to sense her presence. She had begun to wonder if his many acquaintances had taken to alerting him of her whereabouts when she was out in the neighborhood.

The strange draw she felt toward him disturbed her. He was not her idea of someone she could ever love—he was so odd and intense, so rough and overly direct in his manner—and yet there was something about him. She was always glad to see him, but knowing how he felt about her made her nervous. She did not want to lead him on to believe he had a romantic chance with her. She was not going to let that happen.

Her mind stayed fixed on James Wellington. James had finally convinced his father to let him forego a university education in order to stay home to help with the business. Bertie almost wished he had gone off to school so she wouldn't be reminded of him on a daily basis.

But another part of her loved the mere sight of him.

When they passed in the halls, he grinned and sometimes even winked at her, implying that they shared some delicious secret, perhaps that he had once hidden in her room. Bertie couldn't help but smile back. And just when she thought she had quieted her mind from playing the image of his sparkling eyes over and over, another of these chance encounters would set her brain spinning, fixating on his every movement once again.

Bertie finally met J. P. Wellington Sr. one day when she was coming in from an errand. He was a man of about fifty, balding and stout, with muttonchop whiskers around his broad face. The millionaire industrialist asked her name, and she introduced herself.

One October morning, Bertie was racing through the kitchen, almost late as usual, to make it up the stairs into the sewing room. She had arrived at the top floor landing when she heard shouting coming from J. P. Wellington's study. The ferocity of it stopped her cold.

"What is this you've done?" J. P. bellowed. "You've ruined me!"

"I only did what you told me to do!" It was James's voice, shouting back defensively at his father.

Bertie stepped closer to hear, forgetting all about her lateness.

She knew that J. P.'s textile mills down south made fabrics for curtains, blankets, sheets, and other household items, but that he bought the fine fabrics for his fashion line from Europe. He had put James in charge of purchasing the fabrics for this line. His sisters had told her all this while she sewed, since they liked to come to the sewing room to watch her work and to gossip.

Clearly James had mismanaged his task somehow.

Inching a bit closer to the slightly open door, she could see father and son confronting each other: the older one powerful and enraged; his handsome son alternating an aggressive posture with one of near cringing.

Bertie bit her lip anxiously, feeling sorry for James.

"I told you to consult with Mr. LaFleur in Paris before buying anything!" J. P. roared, pounding his wide desk.

"He's an old man!" James shot back. "He doesn't know what young women like. Why should I listen to him?"

"He's only thirty, and he knows what's happening in Paris!" J. P. turned such a bright shade of enraged red that Bertie could imagine his head exploding. "He telegraphed me this morning to say that bolts and bolts of dark gray and blue material have arrived in the New Jersey warehouses. You have spent our entire year's budget on these colors."

"Young women want to look sophisticated, and dark colors make them seem worldly," James defended himself.

"This year women want everything from China!" J. P. argued. "Even if it's not from China, it has to *look* like could be from China! They want dishes from China and rugs from China. And they want *fabrics* from China: bright colors—reds, yellows, purples! They want silken embroidered dresses. LaFleur says all our competitors are featuring them!"

Someone came up the stairs from the kitchen and stood behind Bertie on the hall landing. It was Paddy. "What's the fracas about?" he asked her in a low tone.

She told him what she had heard.

He nodded knowingly. "That lad thinks he knows a great deal more than he actually does," he commented. "I'm happy to see his father putting him in his place."

Bertie scowled at him. He didn't know what James was like at all. "Why are you here?" she asked.

"Mr. Wellington called for his carriage, but I was still feeding the horses, so he asked me to come tell him when I was ready to roll," he explained.

"We are ruined, James!" shouted J. P., his voice thunderous. "I cannot take a loss like this!"

"Send the fabric back!" James told him.

"I can't! Its low price comes with the stipulation that it is not returnable. I've never returned a single bolt in more than twenty years!"

Paddy grabbed Bertie's wrist. There was a dangerous, almost maniacal, gleam in his eyes that frightened her. "Here is our time, my girl! Fate has brought us to this landing at an auspicious moment!"

"Da! No!" was all she had time to say as he pulled her into J. P. Wellington's study. "Good morning, sir," Paddy greeted his employer. "Your carriage awaits outside. But before we leave, I could not help but overhear you speak of your business predicament."

"No doubt the entire block is aware of it," James muttered sullenly.

"Allow me to suggest a remedy for your plight, if you don't mind," said Paddy, releasing Bertie's wrist and stepping forward.

"Go on," J. P. allowed.

"You have met my daughter, Bertie?"

Once again, as on the very first day at the Wellington townhouse, Bertie was seized with an urgent desire to flee, to escape while she still could. What was he up to?

"Miss Miller." J. P. acknowledged her with a nod.

James lifted an ironic eyebrow in her direction, as if to say, *Look at this mess I've gotten myself into.*

"You've seen the excellence of her work aiding

the able Margaret in making dresses for your daughters, have you not?" Paddy began.

"Margaret reports that she is quite skilled and my daughters are impressed," J. P. conceded cautiously.

"Oh, come on, they rave about her," James countered.

Despite the tense situation, Bertie looked down and smiled a bit at his praise.

J. P. glared at his son. "Continue," he prodded Paddy impatiently.

"My talented daughter can take the unsuitable fabric that has been regrettably purchased and transform it into a shining, gleaming dress that will look like it came right over on a boat from China. She will prove to you that it can be done, and then she will show you how to do it on all your dresses."

Bertie's mind was screaming at him to stop talking. He had truly gone insane. She had no idea how to do this! What was he thinking?

"How can she do such a thing?" J. P. questioned.

"We have skills in Ire—Wales . . . such as you have not heard of in this country; ancient spinners and weavers have passed them down from mother to daughter since time immemorial. In no time, Bertie will have your dull colors shining."

"Can you embroider?" J. P. asked, speaking directly to Bertie. "Chinese embroidery is all the rage."

Paddy didn't give her the opportunity to debunk his claims. "Certainly she can. If you give her your pattern books, some of your disastrous fabrics, and sketches of what you'd like to see embroidered on the dress, she will have the most beautiful Chinese-style dress you have ever seen waiting for you in the morning."

J. P. circled his desk, looking from Bertie to Paddy and back again. "We can go to the warehouse and bring back some of the fabric. Miss Miller, you know where the pattern books are kept. I will ask Margaret to give you the rest of the day off to make this dress."

Bertie wanted to throw herself on J. P.'s knees and beg his forgiveness for her father's well-meaning insanity. She longed to say that this was impossible and that it was really not their intention to give him false hope when there was none. "Yes, sir," was all that came out.

"Do you really think you can salvage this disaster?" J. P. asked her.

This was her moment to say, "No!" but nothing came from her mouth.

"She's modest, but I know she can do it," Paddy answered for her.

"All right," said J. P., sitting behind his large desk and taking a cigar from the humidor. "If you can successfully do this for me, my gratitude will know no bounds and the rewards will be great. But if I find that you have wasted my time and my fabric on some foolishness, both you and your father will leave my household immediately!"

∽ ∽ ∽

After leaving the Wellington townhouse, Bertie went directly to the restaurant where Maria worked and, after explaining what she needed to do, asked her friend to stay with Liam and Eileen so she could work all night, because that was surely what would be required, if the task was even possible at all.

"Of course I can," Maria assured her warmly. "How often do you get a chance like this? Go make dresses so heavenly they'll think that the angels created them."

"*You're* an angel!" said Bertie, hugging her.

From the restaurant, she went to the cellar Ray had shown her. With a heavy pattern book gripped under one arm and a carpetbag of thread and needles in her other hand, Bertie climbed down the cellar stairs into the basement room. She had told Da to have a crate of fabric delivered outside the alleyway door, because it was the only place she could think of to work without constantly being interrupted by Liam or Eileen.

She knew J. P. was right about the rage for everything Chinese. She'd noticed the trend coming in the fashion journals the Wellington girls left behind in the sewing room. She'd observed the shift toward rich, jewel-toned, embroidered hats in the bonnets in the Parisian sisters' shop. How had James missed it?

From the carpetbag she took an oil lantern and lit it. The loom and spinning wheel were still there and looked somewhat improved. Ray must have begun working on them.

Going back to the alley, Bertie began dragging down the heavy crate of fabric. It thumped down the first two steps and then got away from her. She jumped out of the way as it slid past her, crashing open at the bottom of the steps.

Hurrying down the stairs, she bent to inspect it. Dark blue material sat inside in a straw packing material that seemed flecked with gold strands. Sifting it through her fingers, she saw it was a mixture of straw and some other kind of gold-colored strips of material. It had probably been added to make the straw softer and less abrasive.

She lifted the blue fabric, holding it out in front of her. It was indeed of good quality, with a slight shine to it, but not at all in fashion.

Sitting cross-legged on the dirt floor that had been strewn with straw, she began to page through the pattern book. The designs were lovely, but she could think of no way to make them work with this material. Her father had promised something shining and remarkable and new. How was she supposed to accomplish *that*?

It was hard to stay mad at Paddy, he was so well-intentioned. She knew he saw this as her chance to advance, to jump forward faster than years of steady toil would accomplish, to catch J. P. Wellington's attention and to dazzle him. But he was such a dreamer!

And now he had put everything in jeopardy: his job, her job. Without either of their salaries, how would they live? It was getting cooler by the day. If they lost the apartment, Eileen would never survive in a mission shelter for the homeless; her health had become so frail.

This was hopeless! She had no idea where to begin. Why even try?

Dropping her head, she let hot tears roll down her cheeks. Crying unabashedly felt like such a relief that she quickly worked herself into a state of full-blown sobbing. Bertie was crying so hard that she didn't hear Ray come down the stairs until he was beside her. "Hey, now," he said, squatting beside her, "what is the matter?"

"Oh, it's such a disaster!" she told him, wiping her eyes.

"Tell me," he prodded.

Bertie tearfully recounted the day's events.

When she was done, he got up and examined the blue material. Then he flipped through the pattern book. He ran his fingers through the packing material, examining it with keen interest. "Do you still have the crimson thread I bought you that day?"

"Yes. I had it in my room at the Wellingtons'. I figured that if I would ever need it, this was the time." She took the spool of shimmering red from her skirt pocket and tossed it to him.

"I can do this for you," he said. "What will you give me if I do?"

"I have nothing," she replied.

He grinned slightly. "You have more than you think. When this is done, we will negotiate the price."

CHAPTER THIRTEEN
Spinning Straw into Gold

The next morning Bertie entered J. P. Wellington's study and greeted her anxiously waiting employer. With flaring nostrils she swallowed the yawn that welled up in her throat. "Good morning, sir," she addressed him, covering her mouth with one hand.

She'd come directly from the basement room, where she had slept for only two hours just before dawn, curled in the corner of the room, while Ray finished his work. She couldn't imagine what she looked like and nervously pushed back some of the curled tendrils that had escaped her frayed hairdo.

The bag she held contained the results of Ray's labor. He'd drawn a pattern in tailor's chalk directly onto the back of the blue material and pinned it using her as his model.

While he had labored on the dress, he'd put her to work picking out the gold cloth from the straw.

She'd worked until exhaustion finally closed her bleary eyes.

Just before she fell asleep, he had been working at the old hand loom. In his lap he held a pile of the gold strips she had sorted out of the packing straw and the spool of crimson thread.

In the morning he'd shaken her awake, thrusting a gown wrapped in the blue fabric into her hand. "You had better hurry," he advised as she'd sleepily brushed the straw from the floor out of her hair. "It's six thirty," he added, looking at a watch he took from his pocket. "I just finished."

Having rushed uptown, sometimes running, she now stood before J. P. Wellington without even having seen the gown. "I see you have brought the dress," J. P. prodded. "Should I call one of the girls to model it?"

"It's fitted to me, as I was the only model available," she explained.

"Then go put it on!" J. P. exploded. "What are you standing there for?"

"Yes, sir." She hurried into the library and locked the door behind her. Freeing the dress from the cloth, she took a swift, sharp breath in amazement.

How had he done it?

Holding the gown out in front of her, she beheld an exquisite strapless evening gown the likes of which she had not seen in any of the sketches in the pattern book. The blue fabric formed the body of the gown, which was nipped in at the waist with a skirt that gracefully draped to the floor.

Appliquéd and embroidered up the entire side of the skirt was a swirling, gorgeous design of Asian-inspired red chrysanthemums.

Immediately she saw that he had used her crimson thread to expertly create the embroidered design.

And incredible as this was, even more spectacular was the crimson cape meant to be worn on top of the gown. The staid blue fabric had been re-created into a luxurious, rich material with a pattern of swirls and lines as if the starry cosmos had been captured within the folds of the fabric. And the pattern appeared to have been woven of pure gold!

But where had he gotten this gold?

A closer inspection gave her the unbelievable answer.

The packing material!

That's what he had been doing on the loom. He'd woven the bits of gold fabric, interspersing them with more bits of the golden thread—and even with the straw pieces—to create this magical cape!

Someone pounded on the door. "We're waiting to see your creation, Bertie," James spoke from the other side. "Are you ready?"

"One minute," she called, delaying him.

As she pulled off her dress, the last pins in her hair came loose and her thick curls tumbled past her shoulders. She would have to pin it back up after she put on the gown.

She stepped into the gown and fastened the cape just as another knock came on the door. "Are you dressed yet?" This time it was J. P.'s demanding, impatient inquiry.

Frantically she clutched at her hair, but there was no more time left. "Yes, I'm ready," she said, unlocking the door.

J. P. and James stepped into the library and circled her. Both looked thunderstruck, and they gazed at her speechlessly.

J. P. stepped closer and took the hem of the cape between his fingers, examining it. "Beautiful," he murmured.

"Yes, beautiful," James echoed, gazing at Bertie as though seeing her for the first time.

Alice, Catherine, and Elizabeth hurried into the library at that moment. "Holy horses!" Catherine cried. "What a dress!"

"Oh, it's divine," Elizabeth agreed. "Is it in your new line, Father? I didn't see it in the pattern book. I must have it. The Autumn Ball is next week. I had a gown I was planning to wear, but I hate it now."

"Bertie is closest to my size," Catherine argued. "Have her make a different one for you."

"Margaret can adjust it to fit me," Elizabeth argued. "It's much too grown-up for you. You're only just making your debut this fall. I simply have to wear this gown."

"Bertie, I need two more dresses of this type, but in styles more suitable to younger girls," J. P. said. "I can give you two days to create them. Can you do it?"

"I don't know, sir, I—"

"If you can, I will give you a sizable bonus. I will also hire you to work alongside James at Wellington Industries for a handsome salary—a very handsome salary, indeed. If not, I will assume that this was a fluke, something you could do only one time, and it will be of no value to me. Your services here will no longer be required, nor will your father's. Do you understand?"

"Yes, sir," she replied.

"Please agree to do it, Bertie," Alice pleaded. "I would so love a dress even half as beautiful as this one."

"Yes! Yes! Please!" Catherine cajoled. "If I can't have this one, I need something like it."

"But I stayed up nearly all night," said Bertie. "I can't do it another night."

"Can she have more time, Father?" James requested. "It's reasonable. The poor girl is only human."

"All right. Today is Thursday. You may take the rest of today and tomorrow and the weekend to work," J. P. allowed. "But I must have the dresses by Monday so they can be fitted properly. I want my daughters to wear them to the Autumn Ball and create a stir. I need a calendar full of orders by the end of the month."

"Do it, Bertie," James urged her. "We would make such a great team."

She nodded, her nostrils flaring once again with a suppressed yawn. "I'll try," she said.

She *would* do it too. For the chance to work side by side with James, she would do anything.

CHAPTER FOURTEEN
Angry Words

Bertie was hurrying home around nine in the morning. J. P. Wellington had told her to go start on the other dresses immediately. She was lost in thought when Ray stepped out of a doorway just before her building. "So?"

"They loved it! You're a magic man!" she said, throwing her arms around him impulsively. "You have saved me yet again. Thank you, a million times, thank you."

He put his hand on her back and rocked her joyfully. "I was glad to do it, princess."

"They want two more, but I'll make them myself," she said, stepping out of his embrace. "I can't ask you to do it again."

"They won't be as good," he said.

Bertie wanted to take offense and call him conceited,

except that she knew he was right. "Your work *is* better than mine. It's amazing, in fact," she admitted. "I truly think you are a genius."

"I know it, though it's always nice to hear," he said with a grin.

"If you wouldn't mind helping me one more time, perhaps this time you could show me how you did it, so that later I could do it myself without asking you for help," she suggested.

"You need sleep," he noted. "Be at the room at seven tonight and we will make two more dresses."

"Thank you," she said again.

"Don't thank me. Remember, we are negotiating a payment."

"Of course," she agreed, without giving her words much thought.

Bertie got home and found Liam sitting in bed with Eileen, showing her the pictures in a book Maria had brought with her the night before. "Maria will be coming back at lunchtime with something called *spag-haddy* for us," he told her.

Eileen stretched her arms to Bertie for a hug. "Ria is nice," she said, her flaxen curls bouncing around her pale face.

The little girl puckered her lips for a kiss, and Bertie kissed her lightly. "How is my girl today?" she asked.

"Eila loves Bridgy," she said with a smile. Bertie took hope from these words. Maybe Eileen was finally improving. She seemed livelier than she had in weeks.

"Liam," Bertie said, fishing five dollar bills from her dress pocket. "Run an errand for me, would you? See if you can find some cod and potatoes for supper. And with the money that's left, go to the thread man and look for the red, shiny thread exactly like the kind I had. Remember the spool of it I showed you? Buy as much of it as you can afford. Tell the man you want crimson thread."

"Sure thing," he agreed, clearly happy to be set free from the apartment for an outing.

"Be back in time for the spag-haddy," she reminded him as he flew out the door.

Bertie played with Eileen until the child went down for her nap. Since she'd become ill, Liam had reported that she slept more than ever. This day it was a relief, since it allowed Bertie to nap beside her.

She awoke with the noon sun blazing in her eyes and Maria shaking her shoulders. "Lunch is here, sleepyhead. I brought you something from the restaurant. Come eat and tell me everything."

Liam ran in with his bag of groceries for supper and poured the change onto the table. "The thread man says he's all out of the crimson thread," he reported.

"Oh, no!" Bertie cried, throwing her hands up despairingly. She swiped the change into her hands. "I'll look later and maybe find something equally nice, though I doubt I'll find anything as beautiful."

With Eileen on her lap, she sat at the table with Liam and Maria and shoveled spaghetti into her mouth. "Slow down. Are you starved?" said Maria, laughing.

"I had no supper or breakfast," Bertie realized. "This is wonderful."

"I told you it was."

They looked at Liam and Eileen, both of whom were completely covered in tomato sauce, and laughed. "Spag-haddy is the best!" Liam announced gleefully.

When Liam and Eileen left the table and began a game of tag around the apartment, Bertie told Maria everything that had happened. "If they like these two dresses, Mr. Wellington will hire me to work alongside James," she concluded.

"The boss's son, the one you've been mooning about after?" Maria asked.

Bertie nodded excitedly. "Maria, I wouldn't be a servant in his eyes any longer. I'd be his partner, his coworker. He said he thought we'd make a great team. Suddenly it might be possible for . . . well, you know."

Maria clapped her hands together delightedly and hummed "The Wedding March." Then she frowned with concern. "But what about Ray?"

"What do you mean?"

"Does he know that he's making these dresses so you can be with the rich and handsome man of your dreams?"

"He doesn't, but I don't see what difference it should make," replied Bertie.

"Of course it makes a difference, Bertie," Maria insisted. "It will make a big difference to Ray. Don't tell me you don't see it. The man keeps helping at every turn because he's madly in love with you."

That night, once again, Bertie left Liam and Eileen with Maria and went out to meet Ray at the basement room. He was already at work when she climbed down the cellar stairs, this time at the spinning wheel. Beside him was a piece of the blue material that had been hacked into with a blade and was almost completely shredded.

"I am spinning it into new material," he explained. He was twisting the blue into the gold pieces from the packing material and even with the bits of straw. The resulting thread was a luminous blend of gold and blue. The straw produced a skein of thread that had body and an unusual nubby texture. "This will be our accent material for the new dresses. Once I weave it together into cloth on the loom, I can use it for collars, belts, cuffs, flounces. No one will ever have seen anything like it; at least not in this country."

"Did you learn to do this as a boy?" she asked.

He nodded. "The cloth making is from my grandmother, yes. People said she had magic hands and that I inherited them from her. The dressmaking I learned from various dressmakers and tailors I've worked for."

"The design of the first dress was so unique," she said. "Did you see it somewhere?"

He tapped his head. "I saw it in here. I imagined it on you."

Watching him work, she remembered Maria's words. Was he really madly in love with her?

Of course he was. He'd made it clear enough.

And did she feel something for him in return?

This was a more difficult question to answer. She felt *something*, to be sure. But what was it? It was certainly nothing that the logical part of her brain could give a name to. He was not what she would rationally desire in a man.

"You are so kind to me," she said, stepping closer to him, and then faltered. How could she possibly tell this man that she could never love him? That was what she needed to say, because it was the right thing to do. But he had been kind, and she didn't want to hurt him.

"You keep telling me you expect payment, but you don't say what it will be," she said, deciding on another approach. "I would feel better if I could pay you and I hope that if I get this job with Wellington Industries, I will someday be able to do so."

"I have money," he replied with a note of irritation as he continued his work. "I don't need your money. I do this for you."

"You know that we will only ever be friends," she said, speaking quickly.

He stopped spinning. "And why is that?"

"Because I don't love you."

He turned and looked at her with that direct,

piercing gaze that made her feel he was seeing into the depths of her heart. "You're wrong," he stated.

She shook her head. "I'm not wrong."

He returned to his spinning. "I can see you more clearly than you can see yourself," he insisted.

She sat on a crate, her head on her hands. What could she do now? She had told him honestly how she felt.

Abruptly, he stopped working and slapped his hand on the spinning wheel. He got up and strode to her. "You know that I love you. I think of you day and night. My feelings for you are real and they are powerful. It must frighten you. It frightens me. You respond to me, too. I can see it in your face, in the way you lean toward me when I am near. You can run from it if you wish, but don't expect me to believe there is nothing between us!"

She stood to face him. Her mind was whirling as if he was somehow hypnotizing her into believing his words. But she couldn't fall under his spell. "I never asked for your help!" she cried. "You helped me because you chose to, but I never asked you for anything!"

He grabbed her by the elbow and pulled her close. "Then give me my payment now. Kiss me, and that will prove to you how much you love me."

She yanked away. "No! I will pay you anything else, but you can't make me feel what I do not feel! What else shall I pay you to make things square between us? Name your price, but it will not be me!"

He laughed bitterly, scornfully. "I don't know. Why don't I take your firstborn child?"

"Ha!" she cried. "Don't be ridiculous!"

"What price would *you* have me name?"

"Fine, then! My firstborn child it is. And when I have money, I will mail it to you and we will be clear of each other, all debts paid, over and done with."

Bertie suddenly felt that she had to get away from him. It was urgent that she not listen to another word he had to say. Overcome with emotion, she ran up the stairs into the alley.

Tears welled in her eyes, but she put her head down and began walking briskly back toward her apartment. She'd known he was hotheaded and rude. Why had she expected anything different from him?

Bertie had walked a block when a horse-drawn hired cab slowed down alongside her. James stretched half out the window, waving to her. "Bertie, hello there! Fancy meeting you down here!"

With the palms of her hands, Bertie dashed the tears from her eyes and forced her lips into a smile.

The carriage stopped and James leaped out, with his friend George Rumpole right behind. He wasn't exactly drunk, but Bertie could see from his unsteady stance that he'd been drinking.

Normally she didn't approve of drunkenness. It was an addiction and scourge that caused only misery, in her opinion. She'd seen it destroy too many lives. But somehow, in James, it didn't seem so bad. He was only out having fun, and he wasn't exactly stumbling drunk.

"I'd have expected you to be holed up somewhere, sewing feverishly. What are you doing down here in this wretched neighborhood?" he asked.

"I might ask the same of you," she countered, deliberately avoiding the question.

"We're slumming—I believe that's the term," he replied with a laugh.

"Pardon?" Bertie had never heard the word.

"It's when the well-to-do avail themselves of the pleasures usually reserved for the low-life denizens of this unsavory area," he said, and she detected the alcohol slur in his voice.

"Do you think it's safe for you to wander about here by yourself, Bertie?" George asked solicitously. "It will soon be dark." She sniffed the distinctive odor of beer on him, but clearly he had not drunk as much as James.

She realized that they had assumed she didn't live in the area and was thankful for their mistake. Meeting them on the street like this made her see how squalid the streets must appear to them, how dangerous and dirty—which, in fact, they were.

"Why aren't you home working on the dresses?" James asked again.

Desperate for something—anything!—to tell him, she recalled some of the fancy ladies she'd seen touring the streets in groups. They glanced in horror at the conditions and spoke loudly about how they would write to the mayor and demand reform. Some stood in front of saloons with signs advocating the prohibition of liquor. Others passed petitions in the street, advocating better working conditions and shorter hours for child laborers.

"I come here as part of my charity work for the poor souls who live in this awful place," she said.

"We knew you looked like an angel, Bertie, but we didn't know you actually were one!" cried George.

"Oh, I'm no angel!" she assured him lightly.

She turned and caught sight of Ray walking fast down the block toward her. His expression was intense, and she knew he was coming after her.

"Can we offer you a lift somewhere?" George asked.

In minutes Ray would be upon her. If he wanted to talk and smooth things out, she should listen to him. But that wasn't what the fierce look on his face told her was on his mind. She certainly didn't want to argue with him here on the street—especially not in front of James.

"Yes, please," she accepted, not even waiting for one of them to open the door for her but quickly climbing into the carriage.

Ray saw her departing and began to run to catch up. James saw it too and shot a concerned glance at Bertie before climbing into the carriage with George.

Ray caught up as the carriage was leaving and was in time to slap his hand on the carriage window. "Bertie!" he yelled.

"Who is that?" asked George.

"Would you like me to get out and deal with him?" James offered eagerly.

Bertie looked down at her hands. "He's someone I know from . . . from my work here. Ignore him. He's probably drunk."

James relaxed in the seat. "Well, nothing wrong with that," he commented with a laugh.

"Where would you like to go?" George asked her.

"I'd like to go uptown to my room at the house," she said. "I need to work, and I can find everything I need there. I can use the sewing machine, and there are fabrics there."

"Fine idea," James approved. "It will be splendid having you at the house. I can see more of you."

"I'll be working," she reminded him.

"I'll keep you company."

CHAPTER FIFTEEN
A Strange Presence Outside the Window

When they arrived at the townhouse, George and James tried to persuade her to go with them to a party, but Bertie declined. Instead she went directly to the sewing room and ripped the top off one of the crates of fabric stacked in the corner. The packing material was just the same as it had been in the other crate. She could use it to make designs now that she'd seen how Ray had done it. She didn't need him.

Flipping through the pattern books, she searched for dresses that would be suitable for Catherine and Alice. At least here she could fit them on their dressmaker's dummies, which would save time in alterations. Plus, she had the sewing machine, which would be invaluable to her.

Lighting the gas lamps in the room, she got to work.

In the morning she was still at her task. Bertie didn't relish the idea of going back to her apartment for fear that Ray would pop out at her when she least expected it, as was his habit. Instead she had Seamus go downtown to ask Maria if she could stay until Monday. "Tell her she's the best friend in the world for doing this," she instructed Seamus, "and someday I will find a way to repay her."

Upon his return, Seamus reported that Maria was delighted to stay, since her own apartment was always noisy and cramped with her parents, grandparents, and eight brothers and sisters all living there. "She says she loves Liam and Eileen, and you never have to think of repaying her."

"She's the truest friend," said Bertie.

"I'd do it myself, but Da has me looking after the horses with him," he said. "Mr. Wellington is going to start paying me a wage too."

"Good for you," she praised him, draping her arm over his shoulders.

"Of course, if you don't do a good job on these dresses, Da says we're all getting the sack," he added.

"I'll do a fine job," she assured him. "Don't you worry."

"I know you will." He smiled at her and then remembered something. "I met that friend of yours, the short fellow with the dark hair."

"Did you speak to him?" she questioned.

Seamus nodded. "He wanted to know where you were."

"Did you tell him?"

"I said you were at work."

Bertie wasn't sure if he knew exactly where she worked. "Did he say anything else?"

"No. He gave me a peppermint candy and left," Seamus reported.

All Friday, Bertie worked while Margaret went about her own task of altering the first dress to fit Elizabeth, on Elizabeth's dummy. She was glad to have Margaret there to advise her. "Don't give Alice a high-waisted dress. It makes her appear chubby," she said at one point. "Raise that neckline on Catherine's dress or Mr. Wellington won't allow her to wear it," she said later.

Before finishing for the day, Bertie could tell that Margaret wanted to talk. She'd been cutting out tissue-paper patterns on the pattern table, but stopped to hear what Margaret had to say.

Margaret perched on a high stool and spoke directly. "Bertie, I hope you realize how important these dresses are to your future. Mr. Wellington is a savvy businessman. He wants to make sure you can reproduce the fine workmanship of the first gown. He values consistency."

"Yes, ma'am. I'm going to do my best."

"Your best was extraordinary on this first gown." She gestured toward the finely made, glistening gown sitting majestically on the dummy. "It has to be every bit as good on the next two."

"It will be," Bertie promised.

Margaret appeared skeptical. "Your work is good, Bertie, but the workmanship on that dress, especially the cape, is remarkable. Even though the seams are hand-sewn, they are as straight and strong as if they were done by machine. The woven thread on the cape looks like it was done by a master weaver. The embroidery is not to be believed. Did you make that dress yourself?"

"A friend helped me," Bertie admitted.

"Will that person help you again?"

Bertie shook her head. "No. We had a bit of an argument."

Margaret drew in a long, slow breath and stood. She put her hand on Bertie's shoulder. "Best of luck, and I will be eager to see the results on Monday."

"Thank you, ma'am." Bertie knew she shouldn't be surprised that Margaret's keen eye had spotted the difference between her workmanship and Ray's much more expert work. But the woman's apparent concern rattled her confidence. These dresses would have to be the best work she'd ever done in her entire life.

Bertie did not leave the sewing room all weekend. James poked his head in from time to time and sat in the large stuffed chair, quietly watching her before leaving just as silently.

One of the serving maids came up with light meals on a tray, a kindness Bertie appreciated greatly. She even slept in the sewing room, sprawling out atop one of the tables for an hour at a time before returning to work.

By late Sunday night, Bertie had two completed

dresses on two dressmaker's dummies: a blue one for Catherine and a dark green one for Alice. They were fine dresses—pretty, well-made, boring dresses.

She had tried her best to make them pop with Asian drama by adding a red sash to Alice's green gown. After her attempts at embroidery had proved time-consuming and unattractive, she'd designed a collage of a crane from various scraps of fabric in the room and had sewn it onto the gown for Catherine. It looked all right, if somewhat childish.

Throwing herself despondently into the large chair, she stared at the dresses, trying to convince herself that she was exhausted and that in the morning light they would seem better than they looked to her at the moment. In her heart she knew it was only wishful thinking. These dresses were simply not good enough.

Sitting there in the chair, she nodded off to sleep but awoke with a start just a short time later, her attention sharply drawn to the window at the far left of the room. Something was outside there, moving on the ledge—a large animal, perhaps. Or a person!

Frightened, she hurried to the window. It was raining, making it hard to see out. To her left, all that she saw was the drainpipe running up the side of the building. Rubbing her weary eyes, she shook her head dolefully. "I'm imagining things now," she said to herself.

Bertie returned to the chair with the intention of coming up with new touches and adjustments that would make the dresses more impressive. With a surge of new hope, she decided that if she worked straight through until the morning she could craft enough improvements to make the dresses more special.

But in minutes, she was asleep once again.

This time Bertie fell into the deep, dreamless sleep of the truly exhausted. It seemed like only minutes had passed, but the sun was soon blazing into the sewing room.

Catherine was shaking her shoulder. "Bertie, you are a genius!" she cried. "Look at these dresses! They're magical!"

Coming slowly awake, Bertie shook her head. "I'm sorry they're not more . . ." With her mouth still open, she let her voice trail off. Her eyes went wide with amazement. She could hardly believe what she was seeing.

On each of the dressmaker's dummies was a dress—but neither was the dress she had made.

Ray had made these dresses. No one else could have.

The one for Alice was suitable for a young teenage girl, stylish yet modest. Its straight lines set off the material that Ray had been weaving when they'd fought. It was blue, heavily interwoven with the gold from the packing material, making an entirely new fabric, one that shimmered. At the dropped waist was an overskirt of gold crochet done in red thread—the crimson thread she'd thought was

135

all used up, or maybe it had been he who'd purchased the last of it.

Catherine's dress was also made of the new, shining fabric but cut into more curvaceous lines as befitted her older age. It was strapless with a flouncing, gorgeously pleated skirt, but what made it spectacular was the short-sleeved, bolero-style jacket. The intricate red and gold embroidery on it depicted Asian blossoms on curving, graceful branches. At the center of each small blossom was a tiny glass bead.

Bertie ran to the window and looked out, as though Ray might still be there perched on the windowsill. He was the one she had glimpsed lurking outside the window.

She saw that the window nearest the drainpipe was not fully closed. A narrow puddle of water pooled there from the night's rain. He'd come up the drainpipe and let himself in. Only he—with his acrobatic carnival skills—could have managed such a feat with a sack of dresses slung over his shoulder.

"Miss Miller, you have done it!" J. P. Wellington said as he stepped into the sewing room. "These are from another world—and I don't mean China! Do you have connections in the faerie kingdom?"

"Maybe so, sir," she replied.

"How do you spin this golden material?" he asked.

She remembered the packing material. "It's spun from straw, sir. It's gold spun from straw."

He smiled pleasantly, assuming she was joking. "Don't fool with me, young lady. I must know," he insisted.

"Truly, it is," she revealed to him. "It's made from the packing material your fabric is shipped in."

"These fabrics are made from that?" he asked incredulously, gesturing toward the open crates.

"It required a loom and a spinning wheel."

"No need for those. Down south I have whole textile factories that can weave this stuff," he said excitedly.

"Mr. Wellington, there is something I should tell you," Bertie said. The time had come to tell J. P. that Ray was the one who had done this. It was his work, and he deserved the credit.

Before she could say any more, James came in. He clapped his hands and grinned at her. "Bertie Miller has done it again, I see."

"I have just learned how she's doing it, James," J. P. said, "and my mind is made up. You and Miss Miller will go south and manage the conversion of all my fabrics into this shining new material."

"You can't ask her to go away with James like that," Elizabeth objected, coming into the room. "It wouldn't be proper."

"I can make it proper," said James. He strode across the room and stooped on one knee in front of her. "Bertie Miller, from the first moment I laid eyes on you I thought you were the most beautiful girl I had even seen," he began. "Now I know you are also a brilliant fashion designer. You and I would make a great team. Will you marry me?"

Elizabeth gasped. Alice and Catherine giggled.

J. P. nodded approvingly. "We could use someone with your talents in the family, Miss Miller," he said. "I'd feel better knowing you were there keeping an eye on James."

Bertie was suddenly sure she was still asleep, her arms draped over the sides of the big cushioned chair. Her humble, boring dresses were still on the dummies, and in the morning she would be promptly dismissed from her position as Margaret's sewing assistant.

She bit her thumb to test if she was awake. It hurt.

Somehow this was all *really* happening.

"Yes, James. I would love to marry you," she replied.

CHAPTER SIXTEEN
Atlanta

The next day Bertie awoke in her small room at the Wellington house knowing what she had to do. She had to tell J. P. who had really made the dresses. It might cost her everything—her new position, her current job, even her engagement to James—but her conscience would never let her alone if she didn't say something.

But then again . . .

Ray might not desire the job or the credit. He was a peculiar person, and it was difficult to say what he might want. Why throw everything away until she knew his thoughts on the matter?

Since her last meeting with Ray had been so charged with anger, Bertie was nervous about speaking to him again. But she had to do it.

She took Seamus with her for moral support. He drove them, with J. P.'s permission, in the carriage that he had recently learned to drive. Bertie had said she needed to get home without specifying where that was.

"I thought this fella was your friend," Seamus said as he opened the door for Bertie. "How is that you don't know where he lives?"

"Because he doesn't live *anywhere* in particular," she explained, "but he's well known around here, and someone will be able to locate him." She felt confident that once she appeared in the neighborhood, he would pop up on his own, as had been his habit in the past. It wouldn't take much looking.

But after an hour of asking for him from the vendors and even in Sullivan's Tavern, they discovered that no one had seen Ray since the day before.

They went up to the apartment to check on Maria, Liam, and Eileen. Liam and Eileen were on the fire escape throwing cupfuls of water on people below and giggling gleefully. Seamus promptly joined in the fun. Maria was baking something called lasagna in the oven, and the place smelled wonderful. She squealed gleefully when Bertie told her of the success with the dresses and of her marriage proposal.

"My, it is touching how that Ray loves you, though, to bring you those beautiful gowns, and even after you two had quarreled," she remarked with a sigh.

"It makes me feel bad. I'm looking for him to at least give him the chance to claim his rightful credit," Bertie said.

"Haven't you heard?" said Maria. "He's left town."

"What?"

She nodded. "I ran into Hilda on the street, and she told me she saw him at the railway station when she was returning from visiting her relatives in Pennsylvania. He was getting on a train."

"Where was he going?" Bertie asked.

"He did not say, or she did not ask—I am not sure which. But he said that he was going for good."

Bertie sighed. Though she was greatly relieved—if he was gone she could keep the credit, James, everything—she was aware of an ache, an inexplicable sense of loss.

He was gone.

Poof! Vanished! Just like that.

Maybe it was because he was the first person she had met in America, or perhaps it was the debt she felt to him—or possibly it was that things had ended so badly between them—but she knew they had unfinished business, and now it seemed it would never be resolved.

It just felt wrong for him to be completely gone so suddenly.

"It is as well that he has gone," Maria said, seeing the anxiety in Bertie's face. "He wanted you to love him, and you know that was not how you felt. I cannot blame you. He was a strange little man. And now you are to marry your true heart's desire with no interference from him."

Bertie nodded. "Of course you're right, Maria."

∽ ∽ ∽

Bertie's engagement to James was announced on the society page of the newspaper: Bertrille Miller of Cardiff, Wales, United Kingdom, to wed James Peter Wellington Jr., son of textile magnate James Peter Wellington Sr.

There was an engagement party to introduce Bertie to society. Margaret whipped up a suitable dress, which Bertie adored. Elizabeth, Catherine, and Alice twisted her hair in the back, fastening it with many hairpins. "This is called a French twist," Elizabeth told her, patting the roll of hair into place, "and it is the height of fashion."

"Leave all the gorgeous curls loose on top and let some wispy strands fall down," Catherine advised. "It's very flirty that way."

"Catherine!" Elizabeth scolded, but with a smile, and did as Catherine had advised.

Just before Bertie was to enter the party room, James caught up with her and slipped his arm around her waist from behind. "You look like a dream," he whispered in her ear.

In early November, James left for the family estate just outside Atlanta, Georgia. He explained to her that because it was outside the city proper and had served as a military base for Northern soldiers, it had not been burned down as the rest of Atlanta had been during the Civil War. "We bought it after the war. It's very old and grand, but a bit creaky and dull. If we want something newer we can move into town," he said.

During the next week, Bertie prepared to leave, packing up her small room at the Wellingtons'. At the same time, things at home were also changing.

There was no point in keeping the tenement apartment now. She'd be taking Eileen with her to Atlanta and Liam would be off to live with Finn, so she informed the landlord that they would leave by mid-November. It had been Halloween the day they received a letter from Finn, saying he had room for his younger brother in the small apartment he'd rented near the firehouse. There was a nearby school Liam could attend. Liam was enthused to join his big brother and to go to school, so it was decided that he should go.

His timing couldn't have been better. But still, Bertie couldn't quite believe they would all be going their separate ways. It made her deeply uneasy.

"My children are all leaving me," Paddy lamented on the day they saw Liam off on the train. "Liam's leaving, and you'll be taking Eileen with you to Atlanta." They had agreed that she should take Eileen, since there would be no one else to take care of her.

"Just for a while," Bertie said as she waved to Liam, who was waving from the window of the departing train. Her eyes were filled with tears. She saw that her father's were as well. "We'll all be together again," she said, and the words caused the tears to overflow, revealing that deep down she was worried that this might not be so. She saw that

Seamus was wiping a mist of tears from his glasses, and she hugged him to her side.

The day she and Eileen left for Atlanta, her father and Seamus drove them to the station in J. P.'s fine coach. "All right, my girls," Paddy said, as they got on the train. "If anyone should give you trouble, find a way to send word to me. Find someone to write you a letter and I'll get someone to read the letter. I'll drive this coach straight to you."

"I love you, Da," said Bertie, hugging him. "Seamus, you take care of this old man. Promise?"

"Sure thing," Seamus promised, quickly wiping under his glasses.

All too quickly, they were on the train and headed to Atlanta. They stopped overnight at a hotel James had booked for them in Washington, D.C., and resumed their trip in the morning. Miles had rumbled on and Bertie now peered out the window of the moving train as the Atlanta railroad station appeared a short distance off.

Eileen was sleeping in the seat beside her, her blond curls spread across Bertie's lap. Bertie felt happy that she breathed easily and was growing stronger every day.

At last the train arrived at the station, and she spied James on the platform. Scooping Eileen into her arms, she left the train along with the other passengers. With sleepy-eyed Eileen in one arm balanced on her hip and her suitcase in the other, she was reminded of the first day, not very long ago at all, that she'd gotten off the steamer at Castle Garden.

Then she'd had nothing but rags on her back. Now she was disembarking from a train to another new land, but this time she was dressed in a fine traveling suit and a chic, feathered hat from the Parisian sisters. The clodhopper boots she'd worn that first day had been replaced with ones that were shining, black, and high-buttoned. Eileen looked like a doll in a flowered frock, her hair in ribbons.

"There are my beauties," James greeted Bertie and Eileen as they got off the train. He kissed Bertie lightly on the cheek. "I'll take you directly to the estate. You'll have a wing of it to yourself, so everything will look quite proper. Our housekeeper will be there. She'll be a sort of chaperone."

He guided them to a waiting carriage. "Father sent a telegram last night and said the dresses were a hit at the Autumn Ball," he reported when they were on their way. "He has pages of orders for dresses made in the same style. We're to begin production immediately. Of course, I'll rely on you tremendously, since you're the brilliant genius with all the talent." He handed her a paper with the orders written on it.

She took it, panicked.

"What's wrong?" he asked.

The matter was that she couldn't read. But how could she tell him that? What would he think of her?

"I'll look at it later," she said. "Right now I'm just a bit weary from the trip."

CHAPTER SEVENTEEN
A New Life

That night Bertie lay in a high, lush, canopied double bed listening to breezes rustling the magnolia tree outside her window. A sheer white curtain blew slightly, and after the constant din of New York City, the quiet seemed odd; though if she shut her eyes, it reminded her of her thatched cottage back home, and she found it calming.

The estate was grand beyond anything she could have ever imagined. The bedroom she was now inhabiting was the size of the entire tenement apartment. Eileen was asleep in the bedroom one door over. She knew she should have been happy that her little sister had such a remarkable room all to herself, but she seemed unnervingly far away.

Fortune had certainly smiled on them. Her wild girlhood idea about being a princess was coming true. Certainly no princess ever lived more splendidly than this.

Somehow she would have to learn to read. There was a fully stocked library on the bottom floor. How fast could she learn?

In the morning she dressed and went down to the dining room, where an elegant breakfast was being served by a very proper if unsmiling staff. Eileen had already been dressed by Mrs. DeNeuve, the house-keeper, in a frilly pink frock under a brilliantly white, ruffle-edged pinafore.

"Good morning," James greeted her. He stood beside the table with a croissant in one hand and a fine china teacup in the other. "I have to go into the office on Whitehall Street this morning. I've asked John, our driver, to take you out to the textile mill to supervise the reweaving of the fabric we have with the packing materials. Father has made a bulk order of your crimson thread, or something like it, so you should be all set."

"But I don't know how to do it!" she said as panic seized her. "I've never even seen a textile mill."

"The foreman, Eustace, knows what to do," he assured her. "You just make sure the result comes out right. Also, the dresses you made are being shipped down, and tissue patterns will be drawn from them. Oversee that, too."

"What will you be doing?" she asked.

"Business things," he replied. "I'll see you tonight."

After breakfast, Mrs. DeNeuve whisked Eileen from her seat. "I've hired a nanny for her," she told Bertie, her voice thick with a Southern drawl. "We have to go introduce ourselves. When you are ready, John is waiting for you at the front of the estate. I have left a sunbonnet for you by the front door."

"Thank you, Mrs. DeNeuve."

When she reached the wide, white-pillared front porch, a man in a formal frock coat came up the steps. "Your carriage," he said, gesturing to the vehicle behind three black horses.

She got in, still tying the ribbon of her bonnet under her chin, and they rode down the very long drive out to the front gate and another five or so miles into the countryside.

Soon they came to what seemed to be another town entirely. This one was nothing like Atlanta, but filled with drab and impoverished-looking stores, a narrow, white clapboard church, and rows of small, identical homes. A sign told her that she had come to the town of Wellington, established in 1870. Home of Wellington Industries.

When she married James, she would be a Wellington—part of a family that owned an entire town!

It was almost too much to take in.

The town gradually sloped down toward a rushing, foaming brown river. The mill came into view as they traveled along the river's banks. It was a gloomy, three-story brick building with several small, dark windows that peered at her like glaring eyes. The second building looming behind it was even larger and more bleak due to its being entirely without windows on the upper floors.

A short, very old man was waiting for them when the carriage reached the front of the mill. John climbed down and opened the carriage door for her to get out. "Good day," the man greeted her formally, without warmth. "I am Eustace Henley, the mill foreman. I have been with the Wellington family since they bought this mill ten years ago."

Bertie introduced herself as the fiancée of James Wellington Jr., which brought only a disgruntled grunt from Eustace. "Thank you for agreeing to show me the mill," she said.

With a curt nod, he beckoned her to follow him into the building they were standing in front of. "This here is the original building that was destroyed by Union troops during the war."

"Your Civil War?" she inquired, remembering what Finn had told her about it one day.

"Yep. The War Between the States is what we call it here," he told her. "This building was rebuilt by Wellington and is now used for carding, spinning, and spooling. The other building that we'll come to is just for carding and weaving."

Bertie followed Eustace through the high-ceilinged, narrow halls of the dark, hot mill. The entire building seemed to throb with nearly deafening sounds of machinery. She trailed him into a huge, open room where row upon row of gigantic machines with moving parts performed different functions.

A row of barefoot, dirty children stood perched on machines, reaching practically into their moving parts. They were no older than Liam. "What are they doing?" she asked.

"They're doffers," Eustace informed her. "They take the full spindles of thread from the spinning frames and replace them with new ones. It's best to use children because they're just the right size to reach the spindles without having to bend."

"The machine is moving and they're right on top of it," she observed. "Couldn't they get hurt?"

He shrugged philosophically. "Some careless ones do. But there are always more to replace them. Most live in town and their parents all work here at the mill, so it's a good place for them to be."

"Everyone in town works here?" she questioned.

"It's a company town," he explained. "The company owns the stores and the houses, and some even say that the pastor of the church answers to J. P. Wellington faster than he answers to God." He snickered a little at his own bitterly irreverent joke. "In Wellington you either work in the textile mill or in the clothing factory down the road."

Bertie knew of mining towns in Ireland where everyone worked for the same mining company, and they were not so different from this town. Once she made the comparison, she understood exactly what she was looking at.

She knew these places employed a lot of people and they were not all bad. But the workers labored long hours and they weren't paid much. They bought everything from the company-owned stores until they became so indebted to the company that they couldn't think of looking elsewhere for a living. After a while, it was as if the company owned their lives.

She smiled at the children, who grinned back at her. One boy was the spitting image of Liam. Tedious though it might have been for him to take care of Eileen, she wouldn't have wanted to think of him, merely eleven, cooped up here near this unforgiving machinery—a soulless monster that would remorselessly rip his arm off if he got too close—placing and replacing spindles of thread all day.

She got to work explaining to Eustace just how Ray had used the packing materials to weave the new fabric. Though she found the man off-putting, he knew his business and seemed to understand exactly what needed to be done and how to do it. "I'll put the littlest girls on this right away," he said. "They're good at picking and sorting, with those tiny fingers they got."

"It's a job they could do outside," Bertie suggested.

"Naw," Eustace disagreed. "They just skip off and start to play if you let them outside."

Bertie figured that was probably true. Who could blame them? They were children, after all.

As John drove Bertie back to the estate, she felt more tired than if she had worked an entire day, though really she'd done nothing. It was as if the textile mill had sucked something out of her. This drained sensation was something she couldn't explain, even to herself, but she felt it.

The thought of seeing James again lifted her spirits when they came up the front drive, but when she got inside, she discovered that he was not yet home.

She met with the nanny, Nancy, a young Frenchwoman about her own age. On a table, Bertie noticed a small stack of books, some in English and some in French. Inside were colorful pictures. "Well, aren't you the lucky girl to have such lovely books," Bertie said to Eileen as she sat with her in the nursery.

"Eila love books," said Eileen, bending down to kiss a volume of Mother Goose rhymes with a loud smack.

"Nancy, would you mind if I looked at the book with you while you read these to Eileen?" Bertie requested.

Nancy seemed bewildered by this, but nodded in agreement. "Yes, miss, as you like."

"Don't call me miss, please," Bertie said. "Bertie will do."

"All right . . . Bertie." She opened the book, and with Eileen on her right and Bertie on her left, she began to read: "Simple Simon met a pieman, going to the fair . . ."

Bertie sat forward alertly, her eyes riveted to every word in the book, determined to learn to read.

CHAPTER EIGHTEEN
A Revealing Conversation

The next two weeks were the busiest that Bertie had ever known. All day she supervised things at the textile mill, checking the fabric that was woven and constantly adjusting it. It was perplexing. The fabric never took on the luminously magical quality that Ray had somehow embedded into it.

It's these machines, she decided one day as she stood in the spinning room watching them work. *They suck the magic out of the thing.* "What if we hired local weavers to make this by hand?" she suggested to Eustace.

He laughed scornfully. "Do that and it will take five times as long and cost ten times as much to make," he scoffed. "You'll miss the season and lose your profit margin."

"What if we only did the trim by hand?" she asked.

"You take that up with your boyfriend," said Eustace, walking off. "I can't make that kind of decision."

That night Bertie waited up for James. She hadn't seen much of him since they came down to Georgia. He would go into the office and not come home until after she was asleep. Every morning at breakfast he promised to return earlier, but he never did. "You are working too hard," she said. In fact, there were circles under his eyes, and he had grown pale and thin.

Now she sat in the rocker on the front porch and waited. She took a banknote from her pocket and put it into an envelope. The amount consisted of the entire salary she had earned to date, plus the hefty bonus J. P. had paid her. J. P. had proven true to his word, and it was a significant amount.

Also in the envelope was a letter to Finn. Since he and maybe Liam were the only two in the family who could read and write, they were the only ones to whom she sent letters.

She was able to do this because Nancy did not mind writing the words Bertie dictated. Since realizing that Bertie couldn't read or write but wanted to learn, Nancy took opportunities to teach Bertie while Eileen napped or played. Nancy and she grew closer by the day. Bertie was glad to have a friend in this big, lonely house.

Now Bertie reviewed the letter she'd dictated, trying to identify the words she recalled speaking:

*My Dear Finn, This is to help you support Liam.
Eileen's and my needs are generously met here, so I have no
expenses, and there is no need to save since I am about to
marry James, who is the son of a wealthy man. I know you
are working, so if there is money left over, please use it to
send Liam to school. I see the children in the mills here and
it breaks my heart to see how hard they work and for so little
money. Many of the young boys remind me of Liam, and I
hope that this money will make it possible for him not to
have to work so that he might finally get the education that
will enable him to have a less harsh life.*

The moon was high in the sky when a hired carriage pulled up to the porch. James tumbled out the
carriage door, nearly falling. She stood to help, but
he righted himself before she could reach him.
"Hello, Bertie," he mumbled, staggering drunkenly
off to the right.

"I thought you were working," she said, outraged
that he was in this condition. "You said you'd come
home early, but you've been out drinking."

He waved her away. "You don't need me here.
You'll do better without me. I'll just muck everything
up like I did when I ordered all that wrong fabric.
You had to save me from that one, didn't you? You're
a smart girl. You handle the work."

"I thought we were supposed to be a great team,"
she reminded him.

"We are," he insisted, throwing himself heavily
down onto the front steps, where he sprawled out,

legs splayed. "You have the brains and talent. I inherit the money. You make me look good and I make you look good 'cause you get to spend my money on dresses, houses, and anything you want. It's perfect."

"But why don't you ever come home?"

"This place is dull. Dull. Dull. Dull. It's more fun in the city."

"Don't you want to see me? We're getting married. I thought you loved me," she said, sitting alongside him on the step.

"Mmmm," he equivocated. "I don't know that I ever said *love*. I thought you were pretty and I wanted to kiss you. But I would never have proposed to a girl like you."

"What do you mean 'like me'?" she asked cautiously. Something inside her had turned cold at his words. Deep down inside, she was pretty sure she knew what he meant, but she wasn't so sure she wanted to admit it.

He laughed thickly, rolling his eyes. "Don't you know, *Bertrille*?" he taunted. "What's your real name, anyway? Colleen? Bridget?"

She gasped. "How did you know?"

"It's Bridget, then! All you girls are named Bridget! Do you think that I never met an Irish servant girl before? The Miller family from Wales! There's a laugh! My father's man might be too stupid to tell the difference, but anyone with half a brain could tell you and your father are Irish. You and I might have had our fling, but I never would have proposed to you if you hadn't worked your magic with those dresses."

"Why are you telling me this?" she demanded, her feelings wounded to their core. "Are you always so mean-spirited when you're drunk?"

He considered that a moment. "I don't know. Maybe I am."

"Well, you needn't marry me," she said indignantly. "I can be employed by Wellington Industries without being married to you." Turning sharply, she hurried into the house and up the stairs.

Throwing herself onto the satin covers of her bed, she sobbed heavily until sleep overcame her.

In the morning she was awakened by a rapping at her door. "Who is it?"

"James. Let me in."

She didn't want to see him and turned on her side with her back to the door without answering.

He knocked again. "Go away," she muttered.

He pushed the door in slightly. "I've come to beg for forgiveness," he stated in a penitent tone.

"Do as you like," she snapped, pulling her blanket up over her shoulder. "I am done with you."

He sat on the edge of her bed. He looked almost yellow, and his eyes appeared sunken. "Bertie, I don't remember what I said exactly, but I recall enough to know that it was probably awful."

"Awful indeed," she confirmed angrily.

"Bertie, don't hate me," he begged pitifully. "It

was the bourbon talking, not me. I didn't mean a word of it."

"How do you know if you can't remember?" she challenged.

"I can tell you're angry with me."

"*That* I am, to be sure."

"I'm sorry, so sorry. I'm so sick that I'm suffering as it is. Don't punish me further."

"You said you didn't want to marry me!" she exploded, "that you didn't love me. You said I wasn't high-class enough for you. What am I supposed to think now?"

"That I was being a drunken fool?"

She nodded vigorously. "Well, yes. Right! I think that for certain." Tears pooled in her eyes, although crying was the last thing she wanted to do. "I'll not marry a man who does not love me!"

"What is love, Bertie?" he asked. "It's a mixture of attraction and respect and mutual need."

"I don't need you," she cried.

"I know you don't," he came back quickly. "But I need you."

She looked at him cautiously. Did he need her?

"It's true. Without you my father just thinks I'm a fool. But you're so brilliant. With you as my wife, he will think of us as one unit and value what we have to offer."

"Oh," she observed coldly, "but you don't value me for myself."

"Aren't your brains part of yourself?" he argued.

"Doesn't your talent and artistry make up the person who you are?"

"I suppose so," she said, conceding the point.

"You see?"

"But do you care for me?" she asked. "Do you love me?"

"Would I be here begging for your forgiveness if I didn't?"

She looked at him uncertainly, not knowing the answer to that question. "And you still want to marry me?" she checked.

"If you'll have a drunken idiot like me," he answered.

"Will you start coming back from the office at a reasonable hour so we can spend time together?"

He raised his hand. "I promise."

"All right, then," she said. "We won't speak of it again."

He grabbed her hands and kissed them. "Thank you, Bertie. You're an angel. You'll see—we are going to make a great team."

CHAPTER NINETEEN
The Last Straw

By December, Wellington's textile mills had rooms and rooms filled with the converted fabric. Rows of seamstresses in the Wellington Clothing Factory down the road were working day and night on sewing machines to make copies of the three dresses Ray had created.

J. P. had depended on Eustace to report to him on their progress. Now he came to see for himself.

"Bertie, my young woman, you have worked miracles," he praised her on the day they toured the mill together. "This effort has put us slightly behind the fashion season, but I have so many orders for your stunning dresses that by Christmas we will have more than made up for it."

"I'm glad you're pleased," she said, and she was. It made life simpler. She was not as impressed with the results. James had advised against making any part of the new fabric or the dresses by hand, claiming, as

Eustace had told her, that it was too costly and would cut too deeply into their profit margin. She argued that the increased value would enable them to raise the price, but he wouldn't hear of it.

To Bertie, the new dresses lacked the exquisite quality of the original gowns.

As she and J. P. stood there, many spindles of red thread spun atop the whirring machinery, feeding down into the weave of the fabric. The young doffers often finished the day with their small hands dyed crimson red from the thread. "The dye shouldn't be coming off like that," she mentioned to J. P. as a little girl walked by, her red hands at her side. "The thread on the originals stayed put."

"Don't worry about it," J. P. dismissed her. "The women who buy these dresses only wear them once, maybe twice. By the time the color starts to wear away, they'll have discarded the dress. We save a bundle by using a lower-quality thread."

"It can't be good for the children to have all that red dye on their hands," she pointed out. "It seeps into their bodies."

"They're young and strong," he said, unconcerned. He walked away, heading for the front door. "Come, let's tour the factory."

John waited out front to take them to the clothing factory. On the way, Bertie took the opportunity to speak to J. P. about something that had been weighing on her mind. "Do you think it is wise to be working the children the long hours that they labor?"

"Who better? They're children. Who has greater endurance or more energy than a child?" he countered. "We follow the labor laws as they exist. Just last year they limited us to using children ten and older, so that's what we do."

"But they're still growing," she argued. "They need light and air and places to play. They need to be in school to learn so they can perhaps get a better job some day."

"What's wrong with working for Wellington Industries?" J. P. asked, coloring slightly with anger.

Bertie also flushed, not with anger but with embarrassment. "Nothing, except that it's hard work for low pay."

"It's unskilled labor," J. P. barked. "Should I pay them the same as educated, skilled people? I think not!"

J. P. was her employer as well as her future father-in-law. She didn't want to anger him. But still . . . she had been practicing what she wanted to say to J. P. since almost the first day she'd arrived. James didn't want to hear about it. She couldn't miss this chance to speak to J. P. now that he was a captive audience in the moving carriage.

"Maybe we could give them some extra breaks during the day and provide snacks for them. It would make them more efficient. It would keep the frail ones from fainting as I've often seen them do. It's very dangerous when they faint on or near the machines. . . ." She shut her eyes and shivered, remembering the horrific result when a little girl had fallen into a moving mechanical part as she passed out from hunger and the heat.

"It might cut medical costs," he said.

"And we could have a school right there at the mill," she suggested.

"How could they work and go to school?" J. P. snapped.

"We could break up their shifts, let them work half days and go to school for half days."

"Bertie, do you fail to realize that we would have to pay them half of what we do now? Their families depend on that money."

"Perhaps we could pay them the same," she suggested timidly.

"For half the work?" J. P. thundered.

"It's mere pennies that they earn," she said.

He sighed irritably. "We'll talk about this another time," he said, putting her off. "The children are sweet and I'm sure you feel for them, but clearly you have no comprehension of the working of economics or of the service we provide these people, who would be starving without the employment we provide."

"No, sir, I don't understand economics," she admitted, very aware of her lack of education. "I only know what a child deserves."

"Believe me, they're getting more than they deserve," he insisted firmly. The carriage rolled into the factory driveway and J. P. turned toward it, leaning to see it from the window. She could tell from his movements that he meant to end the conversation. He slapped his knees gamely as the carriage rolled to a stop. "Let's go see what the women have made of your beautiful dresses," he suggested.

Getting out of the carriage, he walked briskly ahead of Bertie, not waiting for her. With a frustrated sigh, she followed. Clearly, she had not done anything but annoy him with her request for better conditions for the workers.

"James is meeting me here," he told her when she caught up with him at the entrance. "We're a little early, so he may not be here yet."

"Have you ever considered getting one of those new talking machines, sir?" she asked.

"Do you mean that contraption Bell invented?"

"Yes, sir, Atlanta has the wires for them now," she said. Nancy had told her all about it.

"I don't see any wires around here," he noted.

"That's true," she agreed. "I was just thinking that if you had a telephone, you could have called James and told him we were arriving early."

"It's a good idea, actually," he admitted. "We could at least hook up the office in the city. I can see you're going to be a great asset to Wellington Industries. I wish James was as committed to the company. At any rate, don't worry about him. He'll be surprised and delighted to see you. I didn't tell him you were coming with me. Have you set a date for the wedding yet?"

"We've both been so busy we haven't had much

chance to discuss it," she said. At least James claimed he was busy. Despite his promise, he continued to come home late at night, and the long days spent at the mill made Bertie too tired to wait up for him. It occurred to her that maybe she didn't wait up because she simply didn't want to know what condition he was in.

Not knowing made everything simpler.

Eileen was flourishing in this lovely place. Nancy took her outside regularly and read to her under the magnolia tree. The pink had returned to Eileen's cheeks and the sparkle was back in her blue eyes. This was a life Bertie never would have dreamed she could have provided for the little girl.

If she broke things off with James, all this would go away. J. P. might not fire her—though he might. Even if she kept her position, her income would not buy anything like the lifestyle they were living now, not if she were paying rent and buying food and clothing, besides paying someone to care for Eileen.

In her heart, she knew why James didn't break the engagement. He wanted to please his father. He didn't feel he was able to run his end of the business without her help, and maybe he wasn't.

She could imagine how their future would be: They would have little to do with each other but be married nonetheless. It would work out for everyone except that she would never have a man to truly love her. Could she live a loveless life like that? She didn't know.

Her parents had been poor, but they truly loved each other. It was easy to see in every glance, every gesture. Her father always put her mother's happiness before his own, and she did the same with him. Growing up, Bertie had taken it for granted that she would someday know a love as true as her parents had. What a horrible disappointment to think that it now might never happen.

While she was thinking these things, she walked with J. P. into the factory. A foreman hurried down the hall to greet them. "We weren't expecting you so soon, sir," he said apologetically.

"Yes, we're early," J. P. replied.

The foreman handed him a large book. "Mr. LaFleur sent these from France just today," he told J. P. "They're the latest pattern designs from Paris."

"Put them in the back office. I'll look at them later," J. P. requested.

"I'll take them," Bertie offered. "I left a sketch I did for a new design pattern there, and I'd love to show it to you."

"Very well," he said. "Meet me in the main sewing room when you've retrieved your sketch."

Bertie's mind was on her sketch as she hurried to the office with the large book cradled in her arms. It incorporated Chinese chrysanthemums right into the fabric, and she had ideas on how to calibrate the machines to produce a more handwoven quality for it.

She had learned a great deal about the textile trade since coming to Georgia. Making this new fabric excited her, in part because it would be the first creation that was her own and had not been made by Ray.

The door to the office was locked, but she quickly unlocked it and went in. James was seated behind the desk, his blond hair mussed and sticking up in places. One of the seamstresses was sitting on his lap.

The young woman jumped up in alarm.

James smiled. "Hi, Bertie. Miss McGinley here had a nasty splinter in her finger. I was helping her take it out."

Even if Bertie would have allowed herself to be fooled by James, Miss McGinley's guilty, red face proved that he was lying.

James addressed the young woman. "All right, I'm pretty sure we got it, so you can return to work now."

Nodding unhappily, Miss McGinley rushed from the office.

Bertie wanted to shout, even to throw something at him. She could threaten to have Miss McGinley dismissed; maybe she would even do it too.

Then she recalled how charming James had been when she had been the hired seamstress's assistant in the house; how he grinned and winked at her so flirtatiously. She remembered the day he had sneaked into her room, claiming he didn't know it belonged to her. He'd probably known.

James was a handsome, wealthy, dissolute drunkard and an outrageous flirt. He was incapable of applying himself to anything, neither school nor the business. Though she had once thought he was the prince of her dreams, she now saw him as weak, deceitful, and unattractive.

She realized that this growing consciousness of who he really was had been like a wave pounding against a mental dam she'd constructed in her mind to keep such thoughts back. It had been battering at the dam for several weeks. Now the truth about him finally splashed over the top, flooding her mind with new insight.

"We'll speak at home," she said coolly, turning to leave. What was the sense in making a scene?

She was done with him—and this time for good.

James grabbed her elbow to stop her from leaving. "You believe me, don't you?" he asked in an urgent, near whisper.

"Do you really think I am an idiot?" she countered.

"This doesn't change anything between us. She's just a factory girl. It wasn't anything important."

"I'm certain it wasn't," she replied. "I have no doubt that you've done it often before with any number of young women your father hires."

He drew closer to her, and his tone became even more pressing. "You won't tell my father about this, will you?"

The idea of telling J. P. had never even occurred to her. But since he'd brought it up and seemed so panicked by the possibility, she couldn't resist making him squirm: "I haven't decided yet."

CHAPTER TWENTY
A Confrontation

As soon as Bertie returned home with James and J. P., she spied Nancy holding Eileen in the front yard and went to see them. "We have to show you what we found today," Nancy said.

She led Bertie to a bush a small way off. "Birdies!" Eileen cried, clapping gleefully.

Nancy parted the bush's branches to reveal a majestic cardinal's nest made from twigs and leaves woven with red and silken thread. "They're finding bits and pieces from over at the mill," Nancy surmised. "Perhaps you even bring them home on your clothing each day."

"How ingenious they are," said Bertie, impressed. A picture formed in her mind of Ray working at his spinning wheel. He was like these birds, creating beauty with whatever was on hand. She felt a sharp pang of remorse that they had fought and regretted that he had gone away before she could make things right between them. He had been a good friend to her, possibly the best friend she had ever had.

"Oh, I nearly forget," Nancy said, reaching into the pocket of the white apron she wore over her dress. "Mrs. DeNeuve asked me to hold this letter for you. It came today."

Bertie smiled when Nancy handed her the letter. It was from Finn.

"Can you read this to me?" she requested.

Nancy set Eileen on the grass and took the letter, opening it. "Dear Bridget, or shall I call you Bertie? I don't think I will ever get used to that new name.'"

Nancy glanced up at Bertie questioningly.

"Go on," Bertie urged her.

"'Thanks for the money,'" Nancy continued to read.

It will come in handy, since I have lost my job at the fire station. The city cut back on its firefighting force in order to save money. Liam and I will be joining Da and Seamus in a city called Chicago to the west. Once there, we will sign on to lay track for the Transcontinental Railroad. It was completed eleven years ago in 1869, but they are hiring men to keep it in repair. I wrote to Da to tell him where I was headed (Seamus must have read the letter to him. He's teaching himself to read and write, clever lad), and he decided they would join me and Liam. He says old Wellington is too demanding an employer and he wants some new adventure. You will not be able to reach us for a while, since we do not yet know what our address will be. I will write you as soon

as there is a place where you can contact us. Liam is going to school now, but when we leave I will make sure to educate him myself with what I have learned from the nuns and on my own. I hope all is well with you and little Eileen.
Much love from your big brother,
Finn O'Malley.

Bertie took the letter back from Nancy, thanking her.

"So the men in your family will all be together again," Nancy pointed out brightly. "Do you miss them?"

"More than you can imagine," Bertie said wistfully. She picked up Eileen and fluffed her damp curls. The girl was all she had left of her family, at least for the time being. And she was the only one Eileen could depend on.

A lump formed in her throat, and for a moment she lost her resolve. Why break off with James? She had no home to return to now. What if Eileen got sick again?

No. She had to do it. She could not marry a man she had come to despise and one who had no love— not even respect—for her.

They walked together toward the house. Returning Eileen to the grass, Bertie headed up the porch stairs. She would speak privately to James about breaking their engagement, and then they could both inform J. P. together. They could come up with some reason that didn't disgrace James in his father's eyes and just might preserve her position with Wellington Industries. Maybe she could find an apartment in Atlanta and continue to work at the mill.

"Nancy, I might have to move out of here," she said.

"I would miss you," said Nancy, looking unhappy.

"I would miss you, too."

"Why would you leave?"

"Maybe it won't even happen," Bertie said. "But if I got my own place, do you think you could come take care of Eileen while I work?"

"Certainly," Nancy agreed, her face brightening.

When she went inside and arrived at J. P.'s study, the doors were shut. "Have you seen James?" Bertie asked Mrs. DeNeuve, who was passing by.

"He's inside talking to Mr. Wellington Sr.," she said with a nod toward the study.

Bertie sat on a chair in the hall, resolved to grab James the moment he came out of the study. Instead of James, though, it was J. P. who stepped out first. "Ah, there you are, Miss Miller. Please come inside," he said sternly.

Miss Miller? Why was he being so formal? And what was the reason for the cold tone?

"Please, have a seat," said J. P., gesturing to the chair in front of his desk.

Bertie looked to James, but he refused to meet her gaze. What was going on?

"I came down here to discuss finance with my

son. I have noticed irregularities in the company's bank statements, and now he has explained to me the cause of them."

"What is that?" she asked.

"He has informed me that you have been sending money to your brothers in Boston."

"What? Yes, I have—my own money."

J. P. responded with a tight, mirthless smile. "You may have thought that because you were about to marry into the Wellington family, the money was yours to take, but I assure you that is not how I view the situation."

"I only sent the money that was paid to me in my salary and my bonus," she objected.

"There are amounts much more sizable than that missing from the accounts that you and James have control over," J. P. countered.

Bertie looked at James once again, but he still stared straight ahead without acknowledging her. She stood and went to him. "James, tell him that I have not been stealing money!"

"Bertie, remember the night I caught you writing a check out of the accounts book? You assured me you planned to pay it back. Apparently you didn't," he said, speaking at last.

"You liar!" she exploded. "That never happened!"

"There's no sense trying to cover up. You've been caught," he replied.

"It is you who have been taking the money, I think," she shouted. "You have been out every night drinking and probably gambling and fooling around with the factory girls and doing who knows what all else!"

"Is this true?" J. P. asked his son.

"I've been working late at the office, if that's what she means," he answered. "She gets insanely jealous when I have to stay late and hurls all sorts of false accusations at me when I come home after a hard day's work."

"You poor boy," J. P. sympathized. "I had no idea."

"It hasn't been easy, Father."

"It's not true," insisted Bertie passionately. "Just this very day I found him sitting in the office with one of the factory girls on his lap."

"See what I mean?" James said to his father. "I was helping one of the seamstresses who had a splinter. She flies into a green-eyed rage if I even speak to one of the female workers."

"Miss Miller, I cannot have a thief in my employ," J. P. said coldly. "Nor can my son wed a young woman with an unstable temperament." He opened the top drawer of his desk and took out an envelope. "I have some cash here to compensate you for your design work. With it you will be able to afford a train ticket back to New York or wherever you wish to go with your sister."

"You're throwing me out?" she cried.

"I think it would be best for everyone if you left tonight," he confirmed.

CHAPTER TWENTY-ONE
Cast Out

When Bertie came out of the study, she found two suitcases in the front hall: one bag for her and one for Eileen. Mrs. DeNeuve stood beside them, her face expressionless, but clearly avoiding eye contact with Bertie.

"Thank you for packing for us, Mrs. DeNeuve," Bertie said as calmly as she could manage. "I want everyone in the house to know that I never stole a thing from anyone in my life."

"As you say, miss, but Mr. Wellington had me do the packing just to be sure. You're not to return upstairs."

"I have to get Eileen," Bertie protested, anger coloring her cheeks.

"I will send for her," the woman said as she ascended the stairs. In moments she returned with Nancy, who held Eileen in her arms.

"Where we go?" asked Eileen as Nancy tearfully handed her over to Bertie.

"We're getting our own place now," Bertie told her, forcing a smile onto her face.

"I'm so sorry you're leaving," Nancy said, her face flushed with agitation. She hurried to Bertie's side and took hold of her arm. "I wish you weren't going, but I'm glad that you're not marrying that James Wellington. He is not a nice man."

Bertie laughed bitterly. "No, he is not. You are right about that. I'll be in touch when I get my own place."

She realized that her impulsive desire to taunt James, to make him squirm as he wondered what she would tell his father, had backfired badly. He'd decided not to risk having his derelict ways exposed and had vilified her so that anything she might tell J. P. would be suspect. She wouldn't have thought he'd do anything this low. But it made sense, in a way. The new fabric was woven, and the dresses had been cut and pinned and were being sewn. He didn't need her anymore.

"John will take you down to Mrs. Linny's Inn, about ten miles down the road," Mrs. DeNeuve informed Bertie.

The next day she hired Mrs. Linny's adolescent daughter to mind Eileen and a coach to take her into Atlanta, where she would look for work. There was no sense buying a train ticket back to New York, since her family was no longer there and she had no place to live. It seemed more sensible to save the train fare and seek work right there in Atlanta.

But when she began making the rounds of dress-making shops, one question stood in her way: Where was the last place she had worked? They were all impressed when she said it was Wellington Industries, but as soon as potential employers checked this reference by messenger, they learned from someone—probably James—that she had been let go for stealing. That rendered her instantly undesirable.

In the second week, the money was running low. Bertie could no longer afford to pay Mrs. Linny's daughter to watch Eileen, and so she began taking her along on her job search. She tried saying she just arrived from New York City, but without references and with a toddler in tow, no one would take a chance on her.

If only she could find Da and her brothers, they'd send her money and even a train ticket to join them. But if they had written to her, the letter would have come to the Wellington estate, and there was no way she could ever go back there.

In the third week, Bertie ate only enough to keep from fainting and gave the rest of her meals to Eileen. Her clothes began to hanging loosely on her frame. She came down with a deep, hacking cough so powerful that it sometimes made her clutch her side in pain.

"If that's the whooping cough, I'll have to ask you to leave," Mrs. Linny told her when she came upon

Bertie holding her side after a particularly bad bout. "I can't have that contagion in my inn. Everyone will leave. Have you seen a doctor?"

Bertie shook her head as she struggled to catch her breath. "If it doesn't go away soon, I will."

"See that you do."

The next morning Bertie sat at the edge of the narrow bed in her small room at Mrs. Linny's Inn and sighed deeply. She couldn't think of another place to seek work, and there was not enough money left for a train ticket. She now knew she'd made a mistake in staying. If they'd gone back, she might at least be staying with Maria now. Here she was completely friendless.

"What are we going to do, Eileen?" she asked her sister, who sat beside her.

Eileen imitated Bertie's sigh and shrugged her slim shoulders. "Iduhknow," she replied.

"Neither do I, sweet pea," she said, just as another round of fitful coughing seized her. It rocked her frame so violently that it brought tears to her eyes.

This coughing was only getting worse. What if it *was* whooping cough and she couldn't work? How would they live? Who would take care of Eileen?

"Maybe I have to swallow my pride and go to the estate to see if there is a letter for me. I'd rather cut off my arm than go back there, but I think it is our only hope."

Eileen seemed alarmed. "Don't cut your arm. It would have blood."

Bertie laughed wanly. "No, I only mean I do not want to go back there. Don't you worry." She took a napkin off the nightstand and unwrapped the crescent roll she'd saved from last night's supper. She bit off the end, handing the rest to Eileen.

Eileen gobbled most of it down but then put the end piece back on Bertie's lap. "Now you some more," she offered.

Bertie gazed at her fondly. She had been so busy she'd hardly noticed how much Eileen had grown. She was definitely taller than she had been when they'd arrived in America in late summer. "Eileen, you have a birthday coming up soon, don't you, at the end of the month. Do you know how old you will be?"

Eileen held up four fingers.

"Oh, you are a smart girl!" she praised her little sister.

Eileen nodded happily. "Eila four fingers soon."

Bertie took the envelope of money from J. P. off the dresser. There wasn't much left. She should save it for food and rent. "We can walk, Eileen. It's only ten miles." *And ten miles back*, she added silently to herself.

"Eila can walk very good," her sister replied gamely. It was true that she had become much more confident and steady in her walking, having recently shed the toddler's lurching gait.

Outside, the day was overcast with a bitter wind. Despite Eileen's steadier steps, she still couldn't keep up, and it wasn't long before Bertie put her sister on her own back and carried her. Three hours later she trudged up the long driveway to the estate trying to ignore the agonizing blister that had formed at the back of her heel.

On the front porch, Bertie put Eileen down beside her and took a deep breath. "Wish us luck, Eileen," she said as she grasped the door's gleaming brass knocker.

Mrs. DeNeuve answered the door, scowling when she saw Bertie. "Good day, Mrs. DeNeuve. Have any letters come for me since I've been gone?" Bertie asked.

"No," replied Mrs. DeNeuve, moving to shut the door.

"None?"

"Nothing."

"Can I speak to Nancy?"

"She's been let go. Her services were no longer needed."

"Where is she now?"

"I'm sure I have no idea."

"Did they fire her because of me?" Bertie asked urgently.

"Not at all. With no child in the home, there was no further need for a governess," Mrs. DeNeuve said as she closed the door firmly in Bertie's face.

Bertie blinked back tears of disappointment and anger. She had walked so far and for nothing! What was she to do now?

A hard wind blew through the front porch, and she pressed Eileen into her side to shelter the little girl from the blowing sticks and leaves that swirled around them. The maelstrom set off another episode of the choking cough that was plaguing her.

The door reopened just as Bertie caught her first breath, and Mrs. DeNeuve stepped out. "I just recalled that there was one letter two weeks ago."

"Did you see who it was from?" Bertie asked hopefully.

"I did. The return address was from some Irishman named Finn O'Malley in Chicago," Mrs. DeNeuve informed her. "I gave it to young Mr. Wellington."

Her hopes soared! Finn had written to her! He'd left a return address!

"Thank you! Where is James now? Is he at the office in town? I only want my letter, I promise you."

"He's at the mill," Mrs. DeNeuve told her. "But don't go down there. There's trouble."

"What kind of trouble?"

"I'm not sure, but John told me that an angry crowd was forming."

CHAPTER TWENTY-TWO
Trouble

It took Bertie an additional two hours to get to the town of Wellington. Her weary steps grew slower and slower. Several times she had to stop altogether and put Eileen down until her coughing subsided.

When she got into Wellington, it seemed curiously deserted. "Where all the peoples?" Eileen asked from her perch on Bertie's back.

"I don't know," Bertie admitted. Then, though, she spied a crowd milling around in front of a tavern called the Copper Penny. Approaching it, she saw a sign in the window. With a surge of pride, she realized that she could read it: JOIN THE STRIKE! COME INSIDE! HEAR ALL ABOUT IT! FREE LUNCH!

A man barreled out the front door, talking animatedly to another man. "Excuse me," Bertie interrupted them. "What is a strike?"

The man looked her up and down as if he recognized her from the mill, and then decided that this thin, pale woman couldn't be the same one who had managed the mill. "The workers are organizing," he told her. "We've walked off the job until they offer us better pay and decent working conditions."

"That's wonderful," Bertie said.

"It's long overdue," said the other man. "The United Mine Workers have come down to help us organize. The Amalgamated Society of Tailors is here to support us too. Wellington threatened to fire anyone who walked off, but we've banded together: He can't fire everyone in town."

Bertie wanted to say something encouraging, but she was suddenly overtaken with another fit of coughing. The first man she'd spoken to steadied her as she listed to one side. "Say, miss, why not put the tot down and go inside for some of that free lunch? They've got big pots of corned beef and cabbage going. At least you'll be able to sit." He helped lift Eileen from her shoulders and held the door open for them to enter.

Holding Eileen tightly by the wrist, Bertie pushed her way into the crowded tavern. Inside, a wall of heat and the mingled odors of cabbage boiling and body odor from the tightly packed throng assailed her, causing her empty stomach to lurch.

The striking workers were shoulder to shoulder, listening to a fiery speech from a man who stood on a table. Bertie couldn't see over the people in front of her, but she heard the words "organize" and "human rights" and "union," spoken with an accent.

The voice was familiar.

Standing on her toes to see better, she caught sight of the speaker.

It was Ray who was speaking to the crowd!

Bertie jumped up, waving her arm as best she could in the tight quarters to attract his attention. He didn't notice her, so she jumped again.

There was a sharp whistle at the door. Four uniformed police officers strode in forcefully. "This is an illegal assembly for the purposes of promoting civil unrest and a conspiracy to riot!" the tallest officer barked. "You are all under arrest!"

All around her, panicked people began to run. Bertie was pushed in the stampede.

"Stand your ground!" Ray shouted, but it was no use; the need to escape overpowered the crowd, and they were desperate to avoid arrest.

Hanging on to a table to keep from being swept along, Bertie regained her balance once again and stood Eileen on top of the table so she wouldn't be crushed by the crowd.

In the next second, she lost her grip. The moving throng of fleeing people carried her along like a relentless ocean current. "Stay there!" she shouted at Eileen as she struggled to keep her head above the flow. "Don't move. I'll be back for you!"

She was carried out the front door into the street.

Outside stood three horse-drawn police wagons. The struggling strikers were being collared by police and forced inside. In the confusion, many others were running.

Bertie found a clear space to break from the crowd and staggered around the corner away from the mob.

All at once, the miles of walking, the lack of food, the persistent, rib-quaking cough, the crush of the moving crowd—all these debilitating factors converged. Her knees caved and another wave of coughing caused her to buckle forward, holding on to the outside wall of the tavern. The ground below lurched up, tipping her backward.

The last thing she felt was unyielding hardness as her head crashed down onto the ground.

Bertie opened her eyes and peered around. She was on a cot in some narrow, sparely furnished, windowless room. As soon as she turned her head she was slammed with a sickening pain that set off a round of coughing.

A woman in a plain dark blue dress appeared in the doorway. "Ah, you're awake, at last."

Rolling onto her side, Bertie waited until the coughing quieted. "Where am I? What happened?"

The woman, who was only a little older than she, pulled a stool beside the bed and sat. "My name is Emma. I work here at this mission, which is where you are right now. You were outside the Copper Penny, and you must have been knocked down or fainted. You hit your head rather hard, I'm afraid."

"It feels like someone hit *me*," Bertie said, "with a sledgehammer."

"The doctor thought you could have a hairline skull fracture," the woman said.

"How did I get here?"

"Many people passed you by, I'm afraid, thinking you a drunkard who had passed out. But finally a kind gentleman stopped and saw that you were bleeding. The tavern had shut down by then, so he put you in his wagon and brought you here to the mission down the road."

Bertie felt her head and realized it was wrapped in gauze. "How long have I been here?"

"Close to fifteen hours."

Fifteen hours! Bertie lurched forward in alarm, but the pain in her head drove her back onto the bed. "Where is Eileen? Is she all right?"

The woman gazed at her blankly, not understanding.

"The little blond girl who was with me." Bertie's heart began pounding wildly.

The woman shook her head. "They brought you in alone."

CHAPTER TWENTY-THREE
The Real Name

Bertie slept fitfully on the narrow cot, opening her eyes every few hours to ask if Emma had found Eileen. Various strangers came in and told her that Emma had not yet returned from the Copper Penny, where she had gone to inquire. They urged her to sleep more, which she found easy to do.

Several hours later, she became aware of an elderly man in a suit, a doctor, who checked her bandages with amazing gentleness. "Thank you, sir," she murmured with sleepy, half-open eyes. "Have they found Eileen?"

"Emma is not back yet." He lifted a glass of milk to her lips. "Try to get this down. I believe part of your problem is that you haven't eaten. The only cure for that whooping cough is to rest."

The milk caused the churning in Bertie's stomach to stop, but it made her very tired, and she fell back to sleep. When she awoke again, she felt better than she had, though her head was still in agony.

Emma was again sitting by her side.

"Do you have Eileen?" Bertie asked immediately.

Emma sighed. "No, but after much searching I found out who she's with. She was last seen with a man named Rudy."

Bertie sat up in alarm. "I know no one by that name."

"They told me he was speaking to the crowd when you fell."

"Do you mean Ray?"

"They told me his name was Rudy."

"No, it's Ray," she insisted, but even as she spoke a picture was forming in her head. She could see Maria sitting beside her in the sweatshop speaking these words: *That's what he calls himself, but that can't possibly be his name, can it?*

Was Rudy Stalls his real name? Or maybe Stalls wasn't even his real name either.

"What last name did they know him by?"

"No one I spoke to knew it. They only knew him as Rudy," Emma told her. "Honestly, I asked everywhere and everyone I could find. I was told that union organizers like this man often keep their last names a secret so that the heads of corporations and the police can't find them after they leave town."

Bertie remembered that she had once asked him what his real name was, but he had told her it was a secret. If only she had pressed him harder to reveal it.

"Is Eileen with him now?" Bertie asked.

"I couldn't say. Is he a friend of yours?"

"He used to be."

"Then you know where he lives?"

"No. I never knew, and we've not been in touch in some time. Is he staying in Atlanta?"

Emma sighed and looked away for a moment before speaking again. From her pained expression, Bertie could tell she was about to deliver distressing news. "He was seen with her in the railway station very early this morning."

She remembered his enraged words. He'd threatened to take her firstborn child. Eileen was like her own child.

He'd done it! He'd taken her! He knew it was the one thing that would break her heart!

Sick as she was, Bertie staggered from her cot. In her weakness, she had to lean against a wall, but she straightened up as best she could. "I have to find him. Where did they go?" Bertie asked urgently, her heart palpitating rapidly. "What train did they get on?"

"No one knows," replied Emma.

"No one knows?" Bertie echoed Emma's words frantically. "Someone must know. Someone *has* to know!"

This country was huge. Where would she begin to search?

Never to see Eileen again? No! It couldn't be! It was too much to take. It couldn't be happening.

An enormous wave of guilt hit her. She had made this bargain with him. Why? Because she wanted wealth. She wanted to marry James.

She had made this bargain, and now she had lost Eileen, maybe forever.

The terribleness of what she'd done was so impossible to bear that she fainted, crumpling to the floor.

On the third day of Bertie's recovery, she was able to get up. She went to one of the long tables in the mission dining hall and slowly ate a bowl of beef broth that one of the mission workers had brought to her. Each day her head felt somewhat better and her cough was less racking. Bed rest coupled with a steady supply of the plain but nourishing foods the mission served was improving her health, although her mind was fiercely tormented day and night with worry for Eileen.

Emma came in and sat beside her. "I've learned more about this man who was seen with your sister," she said. "I've been talking to anyone I can find who met him while he was here in Wellington. I've learned that he told people he had gone back to using the name he was born with."

"Did anyone know what his original name might be?"

"No, but I've also learned that he went back to New York with her. I asked at the train station, and one of the ticket clerks remembered seeing them."

Bertie hugged Emma. "Thank you for doing that."

"Now that you know those things you can track him down."

"How will I find him?" asked Bertie.

"Detectives, I suppose. It doesn't sound like he is a bad man."

"No. But he is a strange and mysterious man. Once, in a fury, he told me he would take my first-born child in payment for a favor he had done for me. Now I fear that he's done it."

Emma gasped. "Surely not! Eileen is not your firstborn."

"But in a way, she is like my own adopted child. You could say she is my first child."

"Why would he do such a thing?" Emma asked.

Bertie hung her head as tears slid down her cheek. "I suppose he could have done it to be spiteful, because he was angry at me and he knows that Eileen is dearest to my heart. I must find him and get her back, but I don't know where to begin."

"Maybe this will help," said Emma, sliding an envelope stuffed with coins and some cash across the table to her.

Bertie looked at her, confused. "I don't under-stand."

"The people in Wellington took up a collection. It seems that my descriptions made someone realize that I was speaking of James Wellington's fiancée, who used to manage the mill. They'd heard how Mr. Wellington had wronged you and that you were expe-riencing hard times. They told me you were always kind to the workers, especially the children, and so they wanted to help."

"Oh, this is a miracle," Bertie said, squeezing Emma's hand gratefully. "Now I can go back to New York to search for Eileen. I will discover Ray's real last name, no matter what I have to do."

A bitter winter wind blasted up Park Avenue as Bertie was coming from the train station with suitcase in hand. The trip from Atlanta had taken many hours. She'd gotten some sleep on the train but it hadn't stopped her from feeling stiff and exhausted. Every block she walked felt like a mile and the shock of the cold weather didn't help. Bertie stopped to pull her cape more tightly around her shoulders.

A horse-drawn coach in the road began to slow down as if to stop. When it was directly beside her, the door opened. "Bertie, remember me?" said George Rumpole from inside.

"George, hello," she greeted him uneasily. He was James's best friend, and she wasn't sure how much he knew of what had happened.

"Can I offer you a ride somewhere?" he asked.

"If I knew where I was going, you could," she said.

"Then get in, and we'll figure out a destination for you," he said merrily.

She climbed in, pulling her suitcase in behind her. Once she was inside, the driver continued down Park Avenue while she filled George in on everything that had happened in Atlanta with Wellington Industries.

George hadn't spoken to or heard from James since their night of carousing last October. He was not at all shocked to hear of his friend's bad behavior. "James was fun while we were in school," he recalled, "but he's been headed down a bad road for a long time now. I'm sure he gambled away all the money and then accused you of stealing it because he couldn't face his father."

"There were other reasons too," she told him. "I knew things about him he was afraid I'd reveal to his father."

George sighed and shook his head. "I never thought James would go that low," he admitted, "but he's terrified of old man Wellington. He lives in constant fear that he's going to disappoint him so badly one day that he'll cut him out of the will. If that happened he would be lost, because he has no concept of how to work at anything."

Bertie then told him about how Ray had taken Eileen. "Ray is known as Rudy now. He's gone back to his original name. I have to discover his real last name before I can even begin to track him down," she told him.

"I know a detective agency my father uses sometimes in his investment business," George told her.

Ray and Eileen could be miles away by now. There was no time left to be cautious. "Can we go see these detectives now?" she asked.

"Yes," said George. Leaning out the window, he directed the driver to a new address. They went in together and spoke to the detective, Leon Freemont, a short, potbellied man with keen eyes. The man listened while he pulled on his pipe. "I can track this man down easily if he ever used his real name in this country," he said when she was done. "If the trail takes me back to Europe, it will take longer and cost you much more."

"I don't care what it costs," George said. "I have the money."

"Then I'll get right on it," he said.

Outside the detective's office, Bertie and George walked. "Where are you going now?" he asked. "I can get us a coach and take you there."

An idea had come to her, and she gave him the address of the basement where she knew the refurbished loom and the spinning wheel to be. "George," she said. "I want to make you a business offer."

"I have a trust fund at my disposal," he told her. "What kind of business proposal?"

"I want to start a dressmaking business. I'd only need some fabric and thread to start," she said. "It wouldn't be a huge investment."

"Bertie, I saw the dresses at the Autumn Ball, and I know your work is wonderful."

"You haven't seen my work, George. The man I'm seeking did that work. But I've learned a lot from Margaret and even more from working at Wellington Industries. I want to make some dresses and try to sell them."

"You could contact the Wellington girls and see if their friends would buy your dresses," George suggested.

"I couldn't go back there," she protested.

"I could. In fact, I'd welcome an excuse to see Catherine again."

"Ahh, I see," she teased playfully.

He shrugged with a wistful sigh. "She has a new beau, but I've always liked her."

Bertie rubbed his shoulder soothingly. "She'd be a fool not to have you," she said. "Now then, stop with me at some sewing supply and fabric vendors I know of on Orchard Street. We'll buy what we need and I'll get right to work."

After making her purchases with a loan from George, Bertie said good-bye and headed for the alley in the Five Points. From the moment Bertie walked back into that basement room, she knew what she needed to do. It was all there: the spinning wheel, the loom, the open packing crates. Scraps of the dark fabric were still tossed around. There were even scissors and a few pieces of tailor's marking chalk tossed in the corner.

Lying down, she stretched a tape measure from outstretched hand to hand and marked the measurement on the floor. She continued to mark all her measurements on the floor. Now she was ready to make a dress—and to spin golden material from the shreds in the packing material for collars, sashes, bows, and cuffs.

A glint of something red caught her eye. From inside one of the opened crates, she picked up a nearly empty spool of red thread. She recognized the vendor's stamp on top of the wooden spool. It was the original spool of crimson thread that Ray had bought for her so many months ago.

CHAPTER TWENTY-FOUR
Searching for Eileen

Bertie lived in the basement, sleeping on the floor, sometimes wrapped in no more than her cape for a blanket and coming up just to eat. As the weeks progressed from January to February, it grew ever colder in the dark cellar.

Her harsh, barking cough returned, but the dresses were selling well. She would have had enough to rent a proper apartment, but she spent the money on the detective, Leon Freemont, instead, in spite of George's offer.

She did her own searching as well. She sought out Maria at the restaurant where she worked but learned that her friend was no longer working there and that her family had moved from their apartment. She looked for Hilda, but she had gone to live with relatives in Pennsylvania.

Bertie never let George see where she was working but met him at a table in Sullivan's Tavern, where she handed him the latest dresses to deliver to Catherine's friends.

"Does her father know she's doing this?" she asked him one day in mid-February.

"No, but he's in Atlanta most of the time now, so it's not hard for her. All her friends want your dresses," George told her. "Here's the money."

Bertie counted it out and separated it into three piles. "A third for me, a third for you, and a third to invest back into the business for buying supplies."

He slid his pile back to her. "You keep it. I don't need it."

She shook her head, returning it to him. "Partners, remember?" she insisted. "Have you heard from Mr. Freemont?"

"No. I went by his office yesterday, but he told me that he still hasn't found anything," George reported.

As they left Sullivan's Tavern, Bertie heard a bell clanging in the distance and thought of Finn, who had worked on just such a fire truck. The fire truck's blare grew closer, and soon the truck rounded a corner toward George and Bertie. People began to run down the street, passing them by.

One of the running people was Maria. When she spotted Bertie, she came to a complete stop and stared, as though she wasn't sure Bertie was really there. In the next minute, though, she threw her arms around her. "Bertie!" she cried. "Why didn't you tell me you were back?"

"I looked for you but couldn't find you," Bertie told her.

"I moved and changed jobs. I thought you were still in Atlanta."

"Where is everyone going?"

"There's a big fire at Stiltchen's Fabrics."

"Where?"

"It's Ray's new shop. Haven't you heard about it? Of course you haven't. You've been out of town."

"Ray's shop?" Bertie questioned. "But you said it was called Stiltchen's."

"Rudolph Stiltchen—Ray opened the store using that name a few months ago. Apparently it's his real name," Maria informed her.

"Rudolph Stiltchen," Bertie repeated. "And he's opened a shop you say?"

"Well, you may never get to see it. It's on fire, I hear. I was on my way to see what was happening. They say everyone's trapped inside."

"Eileen!" Bertie cried, reeling with the sudden realization that her sister might be trapped in the fire.

By the time Bertie, George, and Maria raced to the corner of Rivington Street, the blaze had reached the sky. Smoke choked the area with gray soot.

"Stay back, miss," a firefighter warned, holding out his arm to stop Bertie as she ran toward the building.

"I have to get in there! My baby sister might be in there!"

But he would not let her pass. Bertie paced like a caged tiger, nearly insane with the need to know if Eileen was inside the shop.

A half hour later, the efforts of the fire department brought the flames to an end. An ambulance arrived to collect the stretchers of customers who had passed out from the smoke. Fortunately, none had been burned.

As the smoke began to clear, a corner shop with a smashed plate window and charred insides appeared. A man covered in soot stumbled out, carefully stepping over the shattered glass left on the window frame.

Bertie ran to him and grabbed his shoulders violently. "Where is she? Where is she? What have you done with Eileen? Tell me or I'll kill you! I swear I will!"

Gripping her arms, Ray held her away from his body. "Hold on! She's fine. She's safe. I've been looking for you."

"You? Looking for me?" What was he talking about?

"You've caught me at sort of a bad moment, I'm afraid," he said, gesturing around him. "But I'll bring you to Eileen."

At a modest, well-kept apartment building two blocks away, Ray, now once again known by his real name, rapped on a first floor door. "Mrs. Kleinbaum, it's Rudolph Stiltchen," he called.

A short, plump, middle-aged woman opened the door and smiled at him. "Oh, you are not burned. Thank God! I was so worried when I heard about your shop! Come. Sit! I'll get you a washrag."

He turned to Maria, George, and Bertie behind him. "I've brought some friends. Is that all right?"

"Welcome! Come in. Come in," Mrs. Kleinbaum greeted them.

Bertie's eyes darted around the apartment as she entered the living room. It was clean and spacious with handsome, if old-fashioned, furniture.

The sound of children laughing rang out.

A boy of about five ran from the dining room around the bend into the living room. Four other children chased him, giggling gleefully.

One of them was Eileen.

She froze when she saw Bertie, her eyes wide with happiness. "Bridgy!" she cried.

Bertie ran to her and, stooping down, wrapped her in a hug as tears of joy ran down her face. "Oh, Eileen, my girl, my sweet, sweet girl!" she sobbed.

George and Maria said good-bye and left together. While Rudy washed in Mrs. Kleinbaum's bathroom, Bertie sat with Eileen on her lap and listened to the woman who had been taking care of Eileen. "Mr. Stiltchen leaves Eileen with me while he runs the shop in the day and picks her up in the evening on his way home," she said. "She's such a good little girl, aren't you, sweetie?"

Eileen smiled at Mrs. Kleinbaum but kept her head resting on Bertie's shoulder.

Rudy came out and asked Mrs. Kleinbaum if he could speak to Bertie privately. The woman lifted Eileen from Bertie's lap and carried her into the other room.

"What happened?" they asked each other at the same time.

"You first," Bertie said.

"I came down to help organize the strike with the Amalgamated Society of Tailors," he said. "When I learned it was Wellington Industries we were dealing with, I went to find you, but they said you weren't with the company anymore."

She shook her head. "I was fired."

"Good," he said. "I'm glad to hear it. You're better off."

"I know."

"I was speaking at that tavern when the police came in and tried to break up our meeting. Everyone fled, and when they were gone, there was Eileen standing on a table. Imagine my shock at finding her there. I went over to the Wellington estate and asked for you there, but they said you had gone. The house-keeper told me you were sick and down on your luck. She seemed almost pleased about it."

Bertie nodded. "Yes."

"I thought that you maybe needed to leave Eileen with me, that you had seen me there and left her behind for me to find."

"So you took her."

"So I took her," he confirmed.

"I fainted just around the corner from the front door," she told him.

He laughed grimly. "I went out the back way with her in order to avoid being arrested. I looked around Atlanta for a day but had no luck. So I came back here, thinking you might return to your apartment, but when I got there it was rented to a new family."

Tears rolled down her cheeks. "And here I thought you had stolen her from me. That you were collecting your debt, she being like my firstborn."

"Why would I do that?"

Her tears came faster and heavier. "Because I wronged you by taking your work and claiming it for my own."

"I offered it to you," he reminded her. "You didn't steal it."

"I should have been truthful about it," she disagreed. "You always said you would collect a price, that we would negotiate my debt."

"And you thought Eileen was my price?" he asked incredulously.

Looking down, she nodded.

He offered her a handkerchief. "All I wanted was your love," he said. "I thought you knew that. When I lost hope of ever collecting that, I spoke in anger. I never expected you to believe I actually meant it. Once you made me see that it was hopeless between us, I needed to get away, to forget all about you. I went to Boston for a while and then Chicago. I got involved with the tailor's union and began to make better money, enough to open the fabric store—the one you just witnessed burning to the ground."

"I'm so sorry," she said. "Now you've lost everything and must start from scratch."

"Not quite everything. Through the union I bought something called insurance. It will pay the money I need to start again."

"Thank heavens," she said. "And can we also start again?"

He put his arm around her and drew her near. In her heart she knew—finally—that he was her dearest friend; he had always been on her side, from the first moment they'd met. His intensity had frightened her, but she understood him now, saw him at last as he really was: a true prince of the spirit.

"I'll always be at your side," he promised.

As she looked into his eyes, she realized that at his side was where she wanted to be, as friends—and much more than friends. She loved him. She suddenly realized that she had loved him for a long time, though her mind had been denying what her heart had always known.

"Now that we've found each other again," he began, "do you think it would be possible that— that—you could—"

He stopped, seeming unsure if he should continue.

"That I could love you?" she supplied.

He nodded. "I have loved you from the start. I think you know that."

"I have been such a fool," she said.

"How?" he asked.

"Not to realize that I always felt the same toward you," she admitted. "Yes, I could love you, I love you already."

A soft smile crossed his face as he pulled her toward him and they kissed. Secure in his arms, Bertie realized that after so much traveling, she had found her real home, the place where she had always belonged.

EPILOGUE

So there it is . . . this faerie's tale of two princesses who lost each other for a while but were happily reunited. It is also the story of a prince from another kingdom altogether, but descended from an equally noble line. They had come to the grand new land to find their fortunes, and find fortune they did.

Paddy and the boys worked their way to California, where they remained with the railroad until 1897. That was the year that Liam and Seamus, young men by then, heard of gold being found in the Klondike River and went up to Canada to find some for themselves. They found enough to make all of them rich.

Bertie's dress business was a sensation. She and George did so handsomely that Bertie soon moved out of the basement workspace into a spacious, light-filled new shop. They hired a team of seamstresses at union wages and paid them generous bonuses if the company's "profit margin" was good that year.

George finally gave up on Catherine Wellington. This was easier for him to do once he met Maria on that day as they all rushed to the fire. In fact, in 1883 he and Maria married. It was the same year that Maria opened her restaurant, Maria's, on Mulberry Street.

The insurance paid Rudy back for most of what he lost—enough, at least, to start again. This time, instead of fabric, he invested in what he knew and loved—tailoring and dressmaking. Eventually the two companies—the one owned by Bertie and George and the one owned by Rudy—merged. They did so well that they surpassed Wellington Industries, which went out of business in 1884, due in large part to disastrous mismanagement by James Wellington Jr.

Bertie changed her name yet again. For the rest of her life she was known as Bertie Stiltchen. Bertie and Rudy married a year after they were reunited and declared their love.

For the rest of her life, Rudy treated Bertie like the princess that his keen intuition had always told him she was. I marked it in my *Book of Faerie*, as is always done when noble members of different kingdoms wed.

They raised Eileen as their own child, in addition to the three sons they had together. She grew into a healthy, spirited young woman. Years later, when she was twenty-four, Eileen went to live with Finn and his eight children in Hollywood because she wanted to be a movie star in silent films. This was a dream she achieved, using the screen name of Laura Miller.

Rudy and Bertie, Maria and George, lived happily in New York City for the rest of their long lives, watching their company's sign flash in the orange setting sun: RUMPOLE-STILTCHEN: SPINNING GOLD OUT OF STRAW SINCE 1882.

And so ends my faerie's tale of an American Dream.

DON'T MISS THIS MAGICAL TITLE
IN THE ONCE UPON A TIME SERIES!

Water Song

SUZANNE WEYN

PROLOGUE
Belgium, April 1915

"What a fool I was!" Emma Winthrop muttered, furious at herself as she stared down at Lloyd Pennington's handsome face in the photo in her opened locket. She sat on a stone wall outside her family's estate with the two halves of the locket open in her hand. When the locket lay open like it did now, it resembled an orange that had been cut in two with its halves side by side. When closed, it was a perfect golden ball worn on a slender gold chain.

She had taken this photograph of him herself and placed it inside her locket. At the time, it had seemed wildly sophisticated to carry a picture of a good-looking boyfriend—one she'd often sneaked out to meet after dark. Back at the Hampshire Girls' Boarding School she used to kiss the photo of Lloyd each night before shutting off her lamp in the dormitory room she shared with four other girls.

The locket had originally belonged to her

great-great-grandmother and had been handed down to her great-grandmother and then to her grandmother and to her mother, who had given it to her. Sometimes it annoyed her when she slept, its round surface digging into her chest, but not even that could compel her to remove it. Back then she'd wanted Lloyd's picture beside her heart at every moment.

How she'd missed him! Dreamed of the day they would be together again. All these months the thought of him had been her only consolation.

And then, yesterday, she'd received a letter from him. A farmer friend of Claudine, the housekeeper, had brought it by. Mail was so rare these days. Hardly any got through enemy lines. She hadn't received word from anyone back in London for nearly five months.

Trembling, nearly weeping tears of joy, she'd ripped the letter open.

But his words slowly filled her with stunned coldness. He'd said that rumors were spreading that her mother had run away from her father, had gone home to her family estate, taking Emma along with her. It was causing quite the scandal in their social circle. No one expected this shocking news from such a socially prominent and respectable family. As a result, his own parents had strongly expressed their wishes that he break off his relationship with Emma. While this pained him, he understood their point. He had to think of his parents and their place in society. He had to consider his future law areer and his possible political future, as well.

Finally, he got to his point: It was perhaps better they didn't see each other anymore.

He apologized for telling her this in a letter. He'd ave preferred to tell her in person, but since she was ow right on the Western Front of the Great War he adn't any idea when she planned on returning.

In conclusion, he hoped Emma would under-cand. It was regrettable, but one had to be realistic nd deal with society on its own terms. It was the vay of the world, after all.

She remembered his words as she continued gazing lown at his photo. How she'd adored him! Now she ouldn't stand to see Lloyd smirking at her for one nore second! The smile she'd once found so irresistibly ttractive now seemed merely smug and self-satisfied.

She swore under her breath in French, a habit he'd picked up in the girls' dormitory at the Hampshire School. "You imbecile!" she snarled at his bicture. "My mother hasn't run away. She hasn't eturned home because she's dead!"

Snapping the two halves of the golden ball shut, Emma hopped from the wall and strode purposefully o the old stone well several yards away. "To hell with vou, Lloyd Pennington, you lying two-face!" she shouted as she hurled the locket. She'd always had a strong throwing arm and acute aim. As intended, the locket sailed into the well.

CHAPTER ONE
The Glowing Green Sky

Emma looked up sharply when the German plane appeared. The sunset of pink and gold filtering into the room had drawn her to the high, arched window. The brilliant quality of the light, so vibrant and yet still, poised between day and night, filled her with a quiet sadness.

But the unexpected appearance of the plane jolted her from her melancholy, diverting her into a state of hyperattentiveness.

Sometimes a lone plane like this was only spying on the Allied troops, reporting back their numbers and position in the field. At least that was what she'd read in the newspapers. In minutes, though, another plane appeared over the rolling fields below, first as a dot in the sky and then slowly coming into clearer focus. She could just barely make out the high whine of the planes' propellers.

Two planes was not a good sign. It meant they

were bombers, not reconnaissance planes. These fighter planes always showed up first, and the strategy seemed to be to bomb from above before attacking with ground troops.

Emma sighed bitterly. It was amazing how much she'd learned about war these last few months. Back at the Hampshire School when she had studied art, music, mathematics, English literature, German, French, and Latin, she'd never have suspected that months later she would become a student of war.

Nothing was more important than war now. In fact, everything else seemed almost ridiculously irrelevant. Back in London she'd pored over the papers, which were full of the war—troop locations; whether they were winning or losing; what nations had joined the fight.

In Belgium she'd learned about war firsthand, seen much more than she'd ever expected or wanted to know. She'd seen things she longed to forget.

Had her parents really thought the Great War wouldn't touch them; that she and her mother could safely visit their family estate in Belgium? How shortsighted that decision now seemed; though back in early September of 1914, her father had been certain all the fighting would be concentrated on the Russian border—the Eastern Front—and Belgium's neutrality would be respected.

He couldn't have been more wrong.

The insectlike buzz of the plane grew louder. Surely they weren't going to bombard the village of

Ypres again. What could possibly be left there that hadn't already been blasted into rubble?

Lately she drifted from one empty day to another here in the huge, rambling estate with only old Claudine and Willem, the manor's caretaker couple, there to help her. Thank god they'd stayed on. If they'd left, Emma knew she wouldn't have been able to cope at all.

She'd been stuck there for nearly seven months, since last September. The seventeenth-century manor house sat right on the line between the Allied French, English, Dutch, Canadian, and Belgian troops and the enemy, the Austrians and Germans. Both sides had dug in to filthy trenches on either side of the fighting. She was right on what had come to be known as the Western Front of the Great War.

The mansion sat on several miles of elevated cliff known as The Ridge. It gave her a perfect view of the trench-torn fields below. It was just like her to be stuck in the thick of things, right smack in the middle of trouble. Only, unlike the schoolgirl mischief she'd gotten into back at the Hampshire School, this was a mess to end all messes—a disaster on a worldwide scale. Some people said it was the end of the world.

It *felt* like the end of the world.

She and her mother should have gone home right away, but then a week later, the German hydrogen vessels, the zeppelins, flew over England and dropped missiles. No one had expected that!

Her father sent a telegram saying it might be

better to stay where they were for the moment. But they'd waited too long. Now a fight had begun to control the North Sea, and the English Channel wasn't safe to cross. The Germans had declared any vessel in those waters fair game for attack. Besides that, she couldn't get past enemy lines in the north.

If only her mother were still there with her.

Rose Winthrop had been too near a missile that exploded in Ypres during an assault on the medieval city. They'd been in a restaurant having lunch. The owner pulled the shutters closed and barricaded the door when the attack began, but the blast tore open the entire front of the restaurant. Emma had desperately mopped blood from her mother's brow and watched the once vibrant eyes grow dull as she slipped away.

It infuriated her to think that people thought her mother had run off, had abandoned her father. It was awful! Why didn't her father set the ugly rumors straight? Hadn't he told people that she had been killed?

It suddenly struck her that maybe he didn't know! Her mother had been buried outside of Ypres. Emma had written her father a letter, telling him what had happened; but maybe he'd never gotten it. She hadn't received a letter back from him in all this time. She'd assumed it was because they couldn't get letters across the enemy lines. It had never occurred to her until that moment that her letter to him had not made it to London.

A knot twisted in her stomach. Did her father think she and her mother had abandoned him? Was that why no one had come to get her?

In the beginning, right after her mother's death, she'd spent every day expecting her father to show up, to console her, to take her home. But he never came. No one came. She hadn't known what to think of this but she'd imagined every possible scenario: her father getting the news and dropping dead of a heart attack; England being attacked and her father taken prisoner; her father being killed in another missile attack. Her imagination spun out endless reasons why he had not come. Most likely, he couldn't get through to her just as she couldn't get to him, but it still didn't stop her from imagining the worst.

This letter from Lloyd meant that her father was alive but not telling anyone that her mother was dead, leaving them to think that she—and Emma—had run off and left him. Was it truly what he thought had happened? If so, how could he think that of them? Her mother would never do that—her loving, good mother—never!

Thinking of her mother made Emma's eyes well with tears. It was so senseless! So stupid! Her mother had died for no reason! Her mother had always been the one she could count on to understand her feelings; the one ready with a hug and comforting words. It was her mother to whom she'd always confided. How she missed talking with her.

And though her mother would have been her

first choice, it would have been a pleasure to have *anyone* at all to talk to these days! Willem and Claudine only spoke Flemish. And, although the sounds of Flemish were a bit like French—and somewhat like Dutch, which was likewise akin, in some ways, to German—she found it nearly impossible to communicate with the couple. Many Belgians spoke German, French, or English. Emma was fluent in all three, having excelled in language at school. Her own mother had been able to speak German and Dutch, being raised as a girl here in the manor. But with Claudine and Willem, it was Flemish or nothing, and so it was nothing.

The rattle of the first round of shelling drew Emma's thoughts back to the planes. Two more fighter planes had joined them, their red and white cross insignias just barely visible from her window.

Her hands flew to her ears, covering them against a sudden deafening blast. The nearest field erupted in white light, shot through with dirt and debris. Even from up here on The Ridge, back a safe distance from the fighting, her window rattled slightly with the impact. The shells were raining down fast now. It always began with a whistle, like ascending fireworks, and then the jarring, bone-rattling explosion. Though she'd heard it before, she could never get used to it.

Staring hard, she tried to see into the trenches out there in the fields. She couldn't detect movement in the long ditches dug into the dirt, but that didn't mean soldiers weren't there, hunkered against the dirt walls, gripping their machine guns, hand grenades, and pistols; waiting, tensely white-knuckled, for the other side to stand and advance first, foolishly exposing itself to their gunfire.

Another shell hit the ground, spraying up more blinding light and deadly debris.

Emma turned away from the window, her face tight with the effort of keeping tears at bay. How much longer could this madness continue?

So many people had died already. Her mother's death loomed larger than all the others to her, but she knew that every death was monumental to someone; every soldier a friend, boyfriend, husband, father, brother, or son. Every civilian and soldier killed was someone's dear one and an irreplaceable loss to that person. And yet the killing went on and on. The death tolls reported in the papers were staggering.

Madness! she thought again. If she heard one more shell fall she might lose her mind altogether.

She crossed the large master bedroom that had once been used by her parents. She'd moved into it because her own bedroom had a leak when it rained and it had been a rainy spring.

The four curved posts of her parents' mahogany bed nearly reached the top of the ceiling. A maroon-colored brocade cloth was draped from post to post. The matching bedcover lay rumpled across the unmade bed.

Emma crawled into it, kicking aside the knotted sheet before pulling her legs into a fetal crouch. Her tears flowed freely now into her pillow, until she had sobbed her way into the relief of sleep.

She dreamed she was having tea with the girls in her dormitory. They sat downstairs in the school's parlor, so happy to be back in the familiar safety of the school once again, back among friends. They were gossiping about someone. She heard their words but couldn't make sense of them. "Who are you talking about?" she asked.

"Don't you know?" asked a girl named Theresa. "It's that Rose Winthrop. She ran away from her husband and then she abandoned her daughter in Europe somewhere—just dumped her and ran off with some man."

"She did not!" Emma objected angrily.

Theresa and the others giggled knowingly. "Yes, she did, silly. Everyone in England knows about it," a second girl named Augusta insisted. "Mr. Winthrop has disowned the mother *and* the daughter, both. He wants nothing to do with either one of them. He has forgotten them entirely and has begun a new family."

"He has not!" Emma screamed, red-faced with humiliation and outrage. "Stop saying that! Stop it!"

She sat straight up in bed, wide awake once again and realizing she'd shouted out loud.

The rapid staccato of machine gun fire now filled the blank spaces between the bombings from above. But something new was happening, something she had never seen before. She noticed it the moment she gazed toward the window.

Swinging her legs out of bed, she returned to the window for a closer look.

Out in the fields, a sickly, greenish-yellow vapor came rising up from the ground. It was like no color she'd ever seen before.

What *was* it?

The ghostly mist seemed strangely evil and filled Emma with an icy dread.

For a moment, both the bombing and the machine gun fire ceased. Her ears adjusted to the sudden silence and she became aware of another sound.

She wasn't certain . . . but . . .

She thought she heard a voice . . . no.

It was many voices.

And they were screaming.

About the Author

SUZANNE   WEYN
is the author of more than a hundred
novels for children and young adults
and has had her work featured on the
New York Times bestseller list. Her other
novels in the Once upon a Time series
include *Water Song* and *The Night Dance*.
Suzanne lives in upstate New York.
Visit her at SuzanneWeynBooks.com.

Need a distraction?

Lauren Strasnick

Anita Liberty

Amy Belasen & Jacob Osborn

Charity Tahmaseb & Darcy Vance

Teri Brown

Eileen Cook

Nico Medina & Billy Merrell

From Simon Pulse

Published by Simon & Schuster

Love is in the air...

♥♥ the romantic comedies ♥♥

♥ How NOT to Spend Your Senior Year ♥ Royally Jacked ♥
Ripped at the Seams ♥ Spin Control ♥ Cupidity
♥ South Beach Sizzle ♥ She's Got the Beat ♥
30 Guys in 30 Days ♥ Animal Attraction ♥ A Novel Idea
♥ Scary Beautiful ♥ Getting to Third Date ♥ Dancing Queen ♥
Major Crush ♥ Do-Over ♥ Love Undercover ♥ Prom Crashers
♥ Gettin' Lucky ♥ The Boys Next Door ♥ In the Stars ♥
Crush du Jour ♥ The Secret Life of a Teenage Siren
♥ Love, Hollywood Style ♥ Something Borrowed ♥
Party Games ♥ Puppy Love ♥ The Twelve Dates of Christmas
♥ Sea of Love ♥ Miss Match ♥ Love on Cue ♥
Drive Me Crazy ♥ Love Off-Limits

From Simon Pulse
PUBLISHED BY SIMON & SCHUSTER

The adorable, delicious—
and très stylish—adventures of
Imogene are delighting readers
around the globe.
Don't miss these darling
new favorites!

A Girl Like Moi

Project Paris

Accidentally Fabulous

by Lisa Barham

From Simon Pulse
Published by Simon & Schuster

Nonboring, Nonpreachy:
Nonfiction

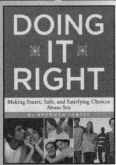

From Simon Pulse | Published by Simon & Schuster

  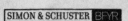